Hidden Agenda

By
Maggie Adamson

PublishAmerica
Baltimore

© 2002 by Maggie Adamson.
All rights reserved. No part of this book may be reproduced in any form without written permission from the publishers, except by a reviewer who may quote brief passages in a review to be printed in a newspaper or magazine.

First printing

ISBN: 1-59129-731-1
PUBLISHED BY PUBLISHAMERICA BOOK
PUBLISHERS
www.publishamerica.com
Baltimore

Printed in the United States of America

For my husband, Douglas Lee Adamson

*With thanks to Kathryn Jensen Pearce and the
Institute of Children's Literature*

Chapter 1

Eliza didn't feel guilty about her plan. Even though she'd be grounded if she were caught, she didn't care. Having endured two months of dull gray days, she was willing to take the risk.

She'd finished her homework in the small conference-cum-storage room of the prestigious Silver Fox Inn, and now she was free to join in on all the excitement of the inn-keeping life. The trouble was, life wasn't very exciting at any central Virginia inn or hotel in late February, but—not to worry—she had a plan. Eliza checked her watch. It was 4:30 p.m. She was right on schedule.

Eliza waited until Harry, a new clerk at the front desk, had disappeared into the kitchen for coffee, leaving Phil, the 'supervisor', seated slumped over with his head down in front of the silent telephone switchboard. She slipped on her coat and, holding her breath, edged past Phil and tiptoed over to the nearest computer terminal. Phil didn't stir as she tapped on the keyboard and the computer went to work with a chink-chinking sound that seemed ten times louder than normal. Eliza spun around as she heard a creak. Whew! It was just a corpulent man in a business suit passing through the lobby, but she was reminded that Harry could return at any moment.

Scanning the screen in front of her, she chose the first vacant room she came across in the one hundred series, which were located on the quietest floor of the hotel. Eliza grabbed a key from the cubbyhole labeled 125 and slipped past the comatose Phil and down an employee corridor leading to an outside exit.

The inn consisted of a main building—including the lobby, guest rooms, conference rooms, restaurants, kitchen, housekeeping and administrative offices—and a detached wing for additional lodging only. There was an icy, penetrating wind outside and Eliza's long, silky brown hair whipped around her as she ran the short distance from the main building to the detached lodge and stepped inside. Trotting down the first floor guest room corridor, she nearly knocked into an elderly lady emerging from her room.

The old woman just shook her cottony-white head, smiled indulgently and muttered, "Children! Always in such a rush!"

On rare occasions, Eliza was grateful for her short stature and her full-cheeked, big-blue-eyed baby face. People gave you a little more latitude if they thought you were twelve rather than sixteen. Bypassing the elevator, Eliza jogged down the carpeted stairwell. As she reached the bottom floor, she glanced at the number on the key clutched in her hand and began searching automatically for the matching door number. Simultaneously, she was busy speculating about what would be playing on Pay Per View.

So far, Eliza had spotted nobody on the lower level. A vacuum cleaner hummed in the background, switching off abruptly. How far away were the vacuum and its human attendant? Eliza jammed the key into Room 123's well-oiled lock and turned. Thrusting open the door, she stepped forward and froze.

On the far side of the room stood a tall, broad-shouldered man with his back to her and his arms around a woman, holding her closely. A long strand of strawberry-blond hair and the ends of a filmy yellow and fuchsia scarf clung to one sleeve of his navy blazer. Eliza stood like a statue in the doorway, her face growing hot with embarrassment at interrupting an intimate embrace. After a long moment, she backed up on shaky legs, shut the door ever so softly and beat a hasty retreat.

It was only when she reached the safety of the main building that Eliza realized she had made not one, but two mistakes. First, she broke a cardinal hotel rule. Always knock before entering a guest room whether you believe the room to be occupied or vacant. Second, as soon as she grabbed the key from its cubbyhole, she should have checked the room number etched on the key against the number inscribed above the cubbyhole. Eliza had heard many a front desk lecture on this very subject. In her haste, she had managed to filch the key to the occupied Room 123 instead of the vacant Room 125 because someone had inadvertently placed the key to 123 in the wrong cubbyhole!

Back at the front desk, the entire upper portion of Phil's body had collapsed over the table in front of the switchboard and occasional soft snuffles emerged. His awkward, stick-thin figure reminded Eliza of a marionette draped heedlessly upon the first convenient surface.

In contrast, Harry was gesturing energetically, as he spoke to a fascinated young bellman. "You shoulda seen her car—a red Corvette. She insisted I drive, and we took off like a rocket..."

Eliza edged past Harry and wandered, seemingly aimlessly, over to the bank of key cubbyholes on the far side of the front desk area. Neither Harry nor the bellman acknowledged or even seemed to notice her presence. Having located the key cubbyhole for Room 123, she kept her eyes trained on Harry as she carefully placed the key in the correct slot. Moving two boxes down, she felt her way inside another cubbyhole and grasped the first key within reach.

The switchboard hummed into life, startling Eliza and

prompting her to slide the key unexamined into her pocket, keeping her eyes on Harry and the bellman. The two men turned toward the noise and grinned at each other as Phil jerked into a sitting position, nearly falling off his chair, and then blearily punched the lit button on the switchboard panel and muttered, "House operator."

Eliza used the distraction to make a fast exit. As soon as she stepped out of the main building, she fished the key out of her pocket. This time, the key did, indeed, have Room 125 inscribed upon it. The chill wind whipped a skein of hair across her face and Eliza sprang into action. As she sprinted past a row of parked cars, she recognized a shiny-new, red Honda and ran all the harder.

Eliza slowed to a fast walk when she entered the building and saw a large group of executive-types approaching. Upon passing them, she broke into a jog and nearly flew down the stairwell to the lower level. She spotted the owner of the red Honda almost immediately. Sydney Sellars was studying the guest room doors, no doubt looking for a hand-drawn star on a 'Do Not Disturb' sign. She and Eliza had agreed that after Eliza secured a room, she would draw a large star on the sign, indicating her presence within. There were a few 'Do Not Disturb' signs but, of course, no stars.

Sydney's honey-blond hair shone, she wore faded jeans and a powder blue, cashmere sweater that flattered her plump, curvy figure and she smiled sweetly, displaying small, perfect teeth, as Eliza approached. "Hey! I was startin' to get worried," Sydney said.

Not wanting to admit to any mishaps, Eliza simply held up the room key. Then she led Sydney down the corridor to Room 125, noticing the 'Do Not Disturb' sign outside Room 123. Too bad it hadn't been there a short while ago!

Before inserting the key in the lock, Eliza knocked conspicuously and receiving no response, she unlocked the door and she and Sydney entered the room. While Eliza stuck the 'Do Not Disturb' sign on their own door, Sydney ran over to the sliding glass doors and pulled the curtains wide.

Eliza frowned. "Come on, Syd. You'll get me in trouble."

Sydney turned toward her. "Relax. There's not a soul out there." Then seeing the anxious look on Eliza's face, she relented.

Eliza felt better as the curtains glided together with a swoosh. "Don't you want to see what's on Pay Per View?"

Sydney walked toward her, smiling sunnily, pulling a cellophane-wrapped packet from her shoulder bag and waving it around. "Popcorn! Isn't that a microwave right over there?"

"Yeah," Eliza said. "Good thinking. Do you mind setting the microwave timer for an hour and forty-five minutes so we can keep track of time?"

While Sydney prepared the popcorn, Eliza reviewed the movie options aloud and they settled upon the one suspense thriller neither had seen before. Each sprawled out on her own queen bed in front of the television, Sydney's popcorn in its original bag and Eliza's stashed in the hotel-provided ice bucket. The twists and turns in the elaborate plot kept them mesmerized until the film's surprise ending. They sat in uncharacteristic silence for a few moments.

When the microwave began chiming, Eliza started and Sydney laughed at her.

"Let's do this again," Sydney said, enthusiastically. "We had our own little movie room. Plus, the secrecy adds an extra thrill."

Eliza nodded half-heartedly and got up to turn off the timer. "Thank goodness I thought about setting the timer. My mom will have hotel employees combing every inch of this place if I don't show up soon."

Sydney rolled her eyes. "My mom was the same way—wouldn't let me breathe on my own. The smartest thing I ever did was to leave Georgia. Dad is great. He knows I can take care of myself."

"He sounds wonderful. I can barely remember my father. He died in a car accident when I was only three years old," Eliza said.

The impudent expression on Sydney's face disappeared, and her lips parted as she prepared to speak.

"I didn't realize you're from Georgia," Eliza blurted, avoiding Sydney's sympathy.

"Yeah. That's where I got this here ac-cent," Sydney said, drawing each word out so that 'accent' sounded like two words, 'ack sent.' Then, she went back to her normal subtle drawl. "Seriously, I moved here two years ago and I intend to stay."

"Still, you must miss your mom sometimes," Eliza said.

Sydney made a face. "Speakin' of moms, didn't you say your mom would send a search party for you if we didn't hurry?"

Eliza sprang into cleaning mode with Sydney as her lackadaisical assistant. After some stray kernels of popcorn were swept up, the beds smoothed, the ice bucket rinsed and dried and returned to its original spot—only the fading popcorn smell spoke of their intrusion. Eliza let Sydney depart first, and, after waiting a few minutes, she let herself out of Room 125 and headed straight for the sales office.

During the short ride home, she rested her head against the cold glass of the passenger-side window and fell asleep, not waking until the car turned off onto a gravel road. They passed the large main house and the barn and, at a fork in the road, headed toward their rented cottage. Sluggishly, Eliza maneuvered herself and her hefty school backpack into the dark, frigid night, stumbling in her haste to reach the warmth of the house.

The next morning was Saturday. Eliza awoke shortly before her 7:00 a.m. alarm, and she shut off the ringing mechanism with a ridiculous feeling of one-upmanship. In half an hour, she and her mother were on their way.

The car followed the winding road past a scattering of new upscale neighborhoods and the occasional horse farm with its neat board fencing before turning left at a large, hand-painted sign, which read 'The Silver Fox Inn.' A row of Linden trees marched along both sides of the drive, proceeding downhill before making a gradual ascent. The fields were a muted green, the Linden tree branches were bare and black against a leaden sky and a punishing wind buffeted their small station wagon.

They reached the crest of the hill, bringing the Silver Fox Inn into full view. The main building was an imposing turn-of-the-century colonial of traditional red brick with half a dozen chimneys and long windows bordered by dark green shutters. Roughly two thirds of the structure was three stories with a gable roof and a gracefully columned, two-story porch, while the remaining third was two stories with a flat-topped roof and parapet.

Eliza's mother gasped. Eliza glanced at her mother sharply, but any questions died in her throat as she followed her mother's gaze past the main building to the pulsing strobes of red and blue light cutting garishly into the misty gray morning. Linda Derby stared anxiously through the windshield as she steered the car slowly toward the three flashing Crown Victorias parked near the detached lodging wing. Eliza's stomach muscles tightened. Something was very wrong.

"Stay here," her mother directed, slamming the driver's side door behind her and approaching the police officer standing near the steps leading down to the lodging wing of the hotel. Eliza waited two minutes before edging out of the car, leaving her own door open a crack and following her mother at a discreet distance.

The police officer was tall and skinny even with a thick wool jacket worn over his uniform. Eliza zipped up her own jacket against the chill wind, tucking her long hair inside the collar. The officer didn't appear to be much older than some of her high school friends. His thin, beaky nose was red with cold, making it stand out in his pale face. He answered her mother's questions mechanically. "A white female in her twenties was found dead in Room 123 this morning."

How horrible, a woman had died. As the words 'Room 123' slowly registered, Eliza's heart leapt. *Please don't let this be the same woman*, she thought. Surely, the woman who died was elderly and feeble. But the officer had just said the woman was in her twenties. A terrifying question entered her mind. Had she interrupted an embrace? Or, she clenched suddenly chattering teeth, had she glimpsed a murder taking place?

Chapter 2

Gradually, from her vantage point a few feet away, Eliza became aware of her mother's questions. "Who was the young woman? Was she the guest room occupant? How did she die?" The police officer ignored Linda Derby's inquiries. Instead, he looked over her shoulder. "Is this your daughter?"

Glancing behind her and shooting Eliza a look that said, I'll deal with you later, Linda Derby said, "Yes, this is my daughter. Eliza, say hello to Officer—" Then, gazing at him with raised eyebrows, "I'm afraid I don't know your name."

"Lewis, Ma'am, Jim Lewis." He removed his hat, fingering the brim nervously. Then, awkwardly but firmly, he steered Eliza and her mother away from the lodging wing back toward their car. "Ma'am, I'm not authorized to answer questions. Detective Thompson has already spoken with your general manager and we'll be interviewing hotel staff later this morning."

Linda Derby came to a halt and shot Jim Lewis a backwards stare. Eliza's mother was barely five feet three inches, but her sophisticated cap of silvery-blond hair, classical yet stylish clothes and, above all, her unshakable air of authority allowed her to dominate the young man.

"I was here yesterday from 7:30 a.m. to 7:00 p.m. Eliza arrived from school around 3:45. Contact me in the sales department when you're ready to speak to me or my daughter," Linda Derby said. Then, turning to face Officer Lewis fully, she added, "There's no need to walk with us any further."

Eliza again followed her mother's figure at a careful distance, hunching her shoulders against the cold. Glancing back, Eliza felt sorry for the young officer as he stared helplessly after them. Linda Derby stalked toward the car and, once they were both inside it, drove the length of the lodging wing slowly before swinging over to the employee lot. When they stepped out of the car, the wind tore at their hair and clothing and didn't cease for the entire fifty-yard distance to the main building.

As they approached the glass double doors, Campbell, the bell captain, saw them coming and held the door open with a beaming smile.

"Good morning, Campbell," Eliza's mother said.

Eliza smiled up at Campbell, the skin around her mouth rigid with cold. There was something reassuring about Campbell's tall, sturdy figure with its slight paunch and his wide smile and gleaming, coppery complexion. Even the bald spot crowning his egg-shaped head had a warm glow. Eliza pictured him in a large, old-fashioned farmhouse with a fat, sweet-tempered wife, and an army of obedient children and grandchildren. She wondered, as she had before, whether Campbell was his last name or his first.

"Good mornin' ladies. That wind is like to kill you," Campbell said. Then his smile vanished. "Sorry. Wasn't no wind that killed that young lady last night."

"The staff know?" Eliza's mother asked him.

"Word gets around pretty quick," Campbell replied.

Eliza's mother shook her head in amazement, yet Eliza knew that she was not truly surprised. Secrets don't last long among the people that work behind the scenes at a hotel. Flashing Campbell a smile, Eliza's mother crossed the dark, highly polished hardwood floors and the jewel-colored oriental rugs toward the front desk, Eliza in her wake.

Her mother caught the eye of Robert Avery, the front desk

manager, and motioned with her head for him to meet her in the small office adjacent to the front desk. Eliza followed her mother and Robert as closely and silently as a shadow. Although she feared her curiosity might, once again, land her in hot water, she wasn't about to miss this conversation.

Eliza thought that Robert Avery must be the most organized person on earth. His clerks rarely made mistakes because they were too well trained and they knew Robert would notice. This made the slip up with the key to Room 123 quite ironic. Even more ironic was the fact that Robert had finally convinced upper management to spend the money to replace the conventional, outdated metal guest room keys with card keys. Since the card key had no number etched upon it and was recoded after every check out, it enhanced hotel security. Plus, a card key would have prevented Eliza from entering the wrong room.

Eliza studied Robert Avery intently. Despite the circumstances, he appeared to be his normal unflappable self. He couldn't have been more than five feet six inches, but from the top of his smooth hair to the polished tips of his shoes, he was meticulously groomed. He and her mother were perfectionists, devoted to the smooth running of the Silver Fox and, thus, the best and most supportive of friends.

Right now, Linda Derby needed information. "This is horrible, Robert. The rookie officer posted outside the lodging wing was unwilling to tell me anything."

"Well, I'll tell you what I know, which isn't much," Robert said in his formal, precise way, smoothing his small, neat mustache. "It seems that housekeeping began their rounds about 6:00 a.m. in the mostly-unoccupied lodging wing. The occupant of Room 123 had arranged for an early-evening checkout, so Amanda Morris from housekeeping was slated to clean the room first thing this morning. When she entered Room 123, the curtains were drawn and there was only a dim foyer light on. Amanda tripped over an object on the floor. After switching on a nearby lamp, she was horrified to see a woman, obviously dead, lying at her feet. Amanda flew from the room, screaming."

"Who was the occupant of Room 123?" Eliza's mother asked.

"A VIP. Paul Dulaney's only child—Fiona Dulaney, a young woman in the custom jewelry business," Robert Avery answered.

"Is it safe to assume the victim was, in fact, Ms. Dulaney?" her mother asked.

Robert nodded. "Most likely. Amanda reviewed the entire incident with me. Fiona Dulaney was a noticeable young woman. Amanda knew what she looked like and she swore the victim was Miss Dulaney."

"Robert, do you know how Fiona Dulaney was killed?" her mother asked, somberly.

Robert shook his head and he and Eliza's mother were silent for a moment.

Eliza felt dazed. She, like Amanda Morris, was familiar with Fiona Dulaney's appearance. She pictured Fiona's long, reddish-blond hair—consistent with that of the woman Eliza glimpsed yesterday in Room 123.

A knock on the door interrupted Eliza's thoughts. Officer Lewis looked younger than ever as he entered the room accompanied by a stately man with silver hair who must have been six and a half feet tall. The older man's heavy, silvery eyebrows; deep-set eyes; jutting cheekbones and long, hollow-cheeked face gave him a naturally somber expression.

He extended a big hand first to Eliza's mother and then to Robert, his mouth turning up in a smile of surprising warmth. "Detective David Thompson. I'll be in charge of the investigation. Sorry to interrupt, but we need to begin interviewing the hotel staff and guests, and the general manager gave us the go ahead to use this room."

Robert and her mother murmured polite acknowledgments and turned to go. Robert strode swiftly from the room, but her mother paused, swiveled back around and stepped forward so that her small figure stood squarely in front of the towering David Thompson.

"Detective, how did Fiona Dulaney die?" she asked.

Officer Lewis, who was already standing near the door, reached out and shut it gently.

Detective Thompson studied Eliza's mother for a moment and, when he spoke, Eliza could barely hear him. "We should receive autopsy results tomorrow. Unofficially—but this is to go no further—she was strangled."

Eliza felt a constriction in her own neck and chest. She rose from the wing chair in the corner of the room where she had faded successfully into the upholstery and cleared her dry throat. The three adults swung around, startled at her appearance.

"There's something I need to tell Detective Thompson, right away," Eliza announced, her voice sounding small and squeaky to her own ears.

Her mother's eyes widened in consternation. "Eliza, what could you possibly have to say?"

Thompson broke in, giving Eliza's mother a reassuring smile. "If you don't mind, I'll go ahead and interview your daughter now, Mrs. Derby."

Her mother nodded hesitantly. "All right, Detective. Eliza, come see me in my office when you're through."

Eliza nodded and watched her mother exit the room. She made a private bet, smiling to herself. If she didn't go by the sales office, her mother would be too busy to notice. When

Mom concentrated on hotel business, she tuned everything else out. Eliza glanced at David Thompson and caught him watching her, his gaze disconcertingly bland.

He gestured to the chairs opposite the desk and, when she was seated, sat down beside her, while Officer Lewis took the only remaining chair behind the desk. "Okay, young lady, what are you so eager to tell me?"

"Yesterday, after I finished my homework, I borrowed one of the room keys, the key to Room 123." Eliza hoped neither man noticed the way her face flushed at the word 'borrowed' and she forced herself to continue. "I thought the room was vacant, but when I opened the door I saw a man with his back to me and his arms around a woman, as if he were embracing her. The only thing I could see of the woman was a strand of her reddish-blond hair."

David Thompson leaned forward so that she could see the intensity brightening his bloodshot, faded-blue eyes. "How far away were you from the couple?"

"I stood in the doorway. They were on the far side of the room in front of the curtains covering the sliding glass doors."

"Can you describe the man?"

Eliza had thought about the tableaux in Room 123 ever since she found out that a woman had been killed there. "From the back, he was kind of a hunk—I mean good-looking. Tall, wide shoulders. He almost totally blocked my view of her. His hair was sort of regular—regular kind of brown, regular haircut..." As Eliza trailed off, she noticed Jim Lewis jotting her words down on a note pad.

Detective Thompson's eyes did not move from her face as he asked his next question. "What was he wearing?"

Eliza was pleased that she could remember without any effort. "A dark blazer—navy blue—and light pants—maybe khaki or gray."

He smiled approvingly. "Good memory, Eliza. Now, think carefully before you speak. Is there anything else you remember? Perhaps about Fiona Dulaney?"

Eliza frowned in concentration. "No. He blocked my view of Miss Dulaney, but it must have been her because I could see some of her reddish-blond hair. I wasn't there very long and I just wanted to leave without them seeing me."

"What about the room itself? Did you notice any objects out of place in the room or clothes strewn about?"

Eliza shook her head. "I think the beds were made and the room was pretty neat or I probably would have noticed, but I wasn't paying attention to the room. I was so surprised to see people..."

Then, Eliza remembered an important detail. "I got out of there in a hurry, but I passed back by Fiona's room about 15 minutes later. There was a 'Do Not Disturb' sign on the door."

Detective Thompson sat up straighter in his chair. "Are you positive the sign wasn't there earlier?"

Eliza nodded vigorously. "Yes. Otherwise, I never would have entered the room."

"Okay. Let's get the timing of all this straight," the detective said.

Eliza not only had to repeat her story several times, but she also had to reveal the details of her plan to watch Pay Per View. The only thing she left out was Sydney's involvement. By the time she finished, her armpits and the palms of her hands were slick with sweat.

David Thompson leaned forward and handed her a business card, speaking softly, his expression more somber than ever. "Eliza— two things. First, and most important, don't talk to anyone about what you saw. It could put you in danger." He let that sink in, before his tense facial features relaxed into a kind smile. "The second thing is—thank you. I know it was difficult to confess to 'borrowing' the guest room keys. You have my card in case you remember anything more, even if it seems insignificant. Again, thanks for coming to us immediately with this information. You did the right thing."

Eliza didn't feel like someone who had done the right thing. An image of the entwined couple flashed through her mind. If only she had looked more closely, she could have determined whether Fiona Dulaney was in danger. She might have saved Miss Dulaney's life! Eliza was swept by a feeling of immense determination. She would do everything she could to help the police find Fiona Dulaney's killer.

Chapter 3

By the time Eliza got back to the front desk, the morning shift was arriving. Her mood lightened the instant she saw Jordan Blake enter with long, sinewy strides, smoothing the dark hair that curled tightly to his head. His teeth gleamed against his tawny skin as he smiled at her, digging in his jacket pocket for his nametag and pinning it dexterously to the front of his navy blazer.

Within seconds, Devin Cooper arrived.

Jordan winked at Eliza and murmured, "Divine, simply Di Vine."

He was right. Devin Cooper was goddess-like from her long, elegant legs; curvy body and lovely facial features to her crowning glory—hair like curling strands of golden silk shot with fire swept into an artful French twist. Devin lit up the cramped, utilitarian space like the first redbuds in a winter-starved landscape.

She gave Eliza a warm smile. Eliza felt a throb of pride and gratitude. Devin—a recent graduate of Sweet Briar College, an exclusive women's school in the nearby Lynchburg, Virginia, area—was always so nice to her, never patronizing despite the difference in their ages. And, it was great to have a female at the front desk for a change. Eliza smiled back at Devin, but her smile faltered midway. Was Devin aware that Fiona Dulaney, her college roommate and close friend, had been killed?

Devin's own smile faded and she glanced from Eliza to Jordan, a puzzled look on her face. Jordan shrugged.

Eliza could see that they hadn't heard. "Someone was killed at the hotel yesterday. Devin, it was your friend, Fiona Dulaney. I'm so sorry..."

Devin stared at Eliza blankly before her handbag slid from nerveless fingers and she buried her face in her hands.

Jordan helped Devin into the nearest chair, giving her shoulder a gentle squeeze. He put an arm around Eliza and led her to the furthest corner. "Why would anyone kill Miss Dulaney?"

Eliza shook her head. "I don't know. The police don't seem to know much yet either. Amanda from housekeeping found Fiona in her room early this morning. Jordan, the police don't want us to spread this around, but she was strangled." Eliza was surprised when her vision grew blurry, her eyes overcome with a sudden hot, moist heat.

Jordan hugged her close, patting her back. "Hey, Eliza, honey. I bet this is the first time you've cried this morning. You've been awfully brave."

Eliza savored the warmth and comfort, inhaling Jordan's subtle, musky cologne along with the more civilized smell of his starched shirt. A year ago, when she and her mother had moved to Charlottesville, Jordan became her first friend. In the beginning, she'd been intimidated by this sleek, handsome stranger. He reminded her of a jungle cat, the way he prowled about the front desk—hazel, gold-flecked eyes glittering.

One day her curiosity got the better of her intimidation. *Why would a man with such untamable energy want to be a front desk clerk?* she asked. To her surprise, Jordan responded with equal candor. *The odd hours of a desk clerk and the occasional lulls that allowed for study were perfect for someone working his way through college*, he explained.

That's how their friendship got started—with her bravado

and his honest and open response. After this conversation, he made a habit of gently teasing Eliza and bringing her into the fold, introducing her to all the staff he'd come to know during his three years plus at the inn.

Despite the affection she felt for Jordan, this was the first time he'd ever hugged her, and, after a couple minutes, she felt awkward. From the hidden portion of the desk where she and Jordan stood, Eliza saw an impatient-looking, middle-aged man in a charcoal business suit approaching the front desk window. She pushed away from Jordan, wiping her face with her fingers and forcing her facial muscles into a smile that felt more like a grimace.

Jordan moved over to the window. "May I help you, sir?"

Automatically tuning out Jordan's conversation, Eliza glanced at Devin. The older girl had pulled out a small mirror from her bag and was applying a fresh coat of lipstick. Eliza was amazed by Devin's self-control. How could she think about makeup at a time like this? As if sensing Eliza's eyes upon her, Devin looked up, her mouth flickering in a small, brief smile. Devin's amber eyes contained just a hint of tears making them appear larger and more lustrous than ever.

Johnny Burnett marched in at just that moment. Tall and broad-shouldered with a clean-cut appearance, he walked like a wind-up toy soldier, stiff and mechanical. He greeted Eliza with his usual distant hello, as if he existed in some stratosphere high above the creatures of the earth, such as her. Eliza remembered vaguely that Johnny's mother came from an extremely wealthy and prestigious family and that some kind of scandal surrounded his deceased father.

When Johnny turned toward Devin, his superior attitude underwent a dramatic transformation. Although still stiffly formal, he became the gallant gentleman, especially when he noticed the tears shimmering in Devin's eyes.

Johnny bent over her chair. "Are you all right? May I get you a soft drink?"

Devin gave him a wobbly smile and a single tear slid down her cheek. "No thanks. I'm okay."

There was a high-pitched hum and a tiny light appeared on the switchboard panel in front of Devin. "Good morning, The Silver Fox Inn, Devin speaking. May I help you?"

There was only the trace of a husky undertone in Devin's voice. Eliza wondered about how the rest of the hotel was handling the situation. She walked quietly over to the heavy swing door leading from the front desk to the kitchen. Just as she stuck out her hand, the door swept open, forcing her backwards.

Robert Avery bustled in. "Hello, again, Miss Derby. I see that Miss Cooper, Mr. Burnett and Mr. Blake have all arrived. Excellent..."

Eliza smiled. That was all that was required because Robert was really talking to himself. Although other managers called staff by their first names, Eliza was accustomed to Robert using titles when he addressed his staff. His old-fashioned courtesy seemed a natural part of his impeccable demeanor. Every time he called her 'Miss Derby' she felt two inches taller. It was as if she were an honorary member of his staff.

She pushed open the heavy door, and this time there was no one coming in the opposite direction. As she traversed the wide hallway leading to the kitchen, her ears were assaulted by a cacophony of sounds—crockery and cutlery banging together, trays being stacked, the whir and hum of numerous appliances in operation, twenty-five to thirty-five voices and pairs of feet competing with each other.

Likewise, when she arrived in the kitchen, her eyes were

bombarded by umpteen ranges, ovens, refrigerators, kitchen gadgets, tables, shelves, white-jacketed kitchen staff and black-and-white uniformed wait staff. The noise echoed off of bare walls, linoleum floors and stainless steel and the harsh fluorescent lights were reflected back by all the shiny, bare surfaces. The odors of half a dozen dishes being prepared and cooked gave the air a unique pungency, while the heat from the ovens caused her own temperature to rise.

Despite the heat, Eliza was energized by the activity. At the same time the familiarity of it all brought her a certain comfort. The tension and somberness enveloping her was eased. Dodging the paths of the bustling kitchen and wait staff, she headed for the stainless-steel soft drink dispenser.

The dispenser was near the kitchen entrance to the formal dining room where a circle of wait staff had congregated. Eliza selected a cup from the stacked tier of glasses, concentrating on the wait staff's conversation rather than her beverage.

A short girl with streaky-blond hair was talking animatedly. "I served Fiona Dulaney lobster bisque yesterday. She sent me back to the kitchen to warm it up. Then she ordered a salad, but we had to, like, leave out half the ingredients and put the dressing on the side for her royal highness. She was, like, so-o-o picky."

A skinny, prune-faced brunette responded, every line on her face etched with sour cynicism, "Yeah, well, now we have one less picky woman to deal with."

There was a sputter of laughter which died down uneasily. Eliza was stunned by how lightly they were taking the murder. Then she studied their faces and realized that—notwithstanding the blond and the prune-faced woman—shock and fear lurked just below the surface.

Eliza screwed up her own courage. "Who was eating with

Miss Dulaney?"

The wait staff shot her varying looks of surprise or disapproval, as if they either hadn't seen Eliza or they believed that, like all well-trained children, she should be seen but not heard. For the zillionth time, she wished she were tall with cheekbones, instead of five feet two with chipmunk cheeks.

Eliza cleared her throat. "Was Miss Dulaney eating by herself?"

Everyone turned toward the blond curiously. "No," she said and paused, drawing the moment out. "She was with a man—a tall, tan outdoors type with a sweet face—kind of like that actor, Brad Pitt, only taller."

Eliza felt a spurt of excitement. "Did you get the feeling the guy was her boyfriend?"

The others were perfectly silent, wanting to hear the answer. "Well, they weren't, like, holding hands and calling each other 'honey', but she was attracted. You could tell by the way she smiled... He was harder to read, but she did, like, watch his every move."

Eliza stepped closer so she could read the waitress' nametag. "Maureen, did you catch any of their conversation?"

Maureen laughed and glanced at the others, rolling her eyes at this nosy kid. "Sweetie, there were, like, two wait persons in the whole restaurant that day, me and a guy who just got moved up from busboy. It was s'posed to be quiet but you coulda fooled me. Even if I wanted to, I was wa-a-ay too busy to listen in on what people were saying to each other."

Several of the wait staff nodded their heads empathetically. A few glanced at Eliza with mild disdain and others, having lost interest, turned away.

Eliza searched her brain feverishly. Was there anything else she should ask? She slapped herself, mentally. *Of course!* "What was this Brad Pitt guy wearing?"

Maureen sighed, giving Eliza a look of exaggerated patience. "How am I s'posed to remem—" She paused, her irritatingly patient look vanished and she nodded her head in approval at her own remarkable memory. "He wore one of those, like, off-white fisherman's sweaters. You know, the kind that are made in Scotland or England. He looked, like, so macho in that sweater, I thought I'd get one for my boyfriend."

Eliza had been hoping to hear about a navy blazer, but she hid her disappointment. "Wow! I can't believe how good your memory is. Do you happen to remember what kind of pants he was wearing?"

Now that her gifts as an observer had been praised, Maureen was trying harder to be helpful. She paused to think, but then shook her head. Eliza thanked her profusely and, from the corner of her eyes, caught the approach of the headwaiter, a man with a hair-trigger temper. She edged back over to the soft drink dispenser and filled up her empty glass with ice and Dr. Pepper.

Eliza's heart was beating rapidly. It was exhilarating to feel that she was hot on the trail. On the very day that Fiona was murdered, she'd had lunch with a mystery man. But Maureen's description of the mysterious lunch partner/a.k.a. Brad Pitt didn't quite match Eliza's memory of the possible killer. Unless Brad Pitt wore a blazer over his sweater. As Eliza's heartbeat slowed to normal, she experienced a feeling of let down. Finding Fiona Dulaney's killer would not be easy.

Sipping her drink, Eliza felt an urge to go see her mother as requested after all. On her way out of the kitchen, she grabbed a couple of homemade cookies. She walked past the food and beverage office and entered a windowless steel door on the left. Her feet clattered on the concrete stairs and echoed off the cinderblock walls. The fluorescent lights shone harshly on the gray paint, and the air was redolent with the musty odors of dust and metal. A door squeaked open somewhere above her, a metallic object fell, there was some shuffling and, soon after, the loud echo of footsteps descending.

Suddenly, Eliza just wanted to get out of the stairwell. She cursed herself for bringing the cookies and Dr. Pepper, but she'd feel silly if she just abandoned them on the stairs. Hardly noticing the ache in her arms and legs, she climbed as swiftly and silently as she could.

Just as Eliza reached the second-story landing, a pair of black shoes and stockings followed by a black skirt, white blouse and small tray of dirty crockery descended from above. Here was Eliza's imagined predator, a woman on the banquet staff doubtless serving in the third-floor conference rooms. Looking at the woman's pale, cosmetic-free face and the strands of graying brown hair that had escaped their neat knot, Eliza felt foolish. She smiled in greeting and the woman smiled wanly in return, continuing her downward journey. Still, Eliza was relieved when she stepped out of the stairwell onto the second floor.

Fear seemed to have heightened her senses. As she trod down the corridor, she noticed the utter silence. The carpet was soft and plush beneath her feet, the delicate fleur-de-lis patterned wallpaper shimmered like satin and the wall sconces shone with a soft, subtle light. The paintings; the small, highly polished tables adorned with vases of fresh flowers or porcelain bowls of sweetly-scented potpourri; the antique look of the occasional mirror or chair all contributed to a sense of well-being and leisure.

Eliza was struck by the contrast between the inn's employee areas and the guest areas. In the past she had taken it for granted, whereas now she realized how strange it must be to work day after day in a place you would never dream of staying in yourself—even for your honeymoon! Yet, many of the Silver Fox's guests were frequent visitors who thought nothing of staying two weeks or more. Fiona Dulaney had been a regular guest, and her clothes and jewelry bespoke a life of pampered luxury. Was Fiona's killer someone who resented her lifestyle?

Having reached a door with a large window and underneath a brass plate spelling out 'Sales Office', Eliza entered, smiling at the three well dressed young women behind their handsome, mahogany desks. She strode past their desks and through an open door to a smaller room with a beautiful pair of floor-to-ceiling windows. Her mother leaned over her desk, jotting notes on a thick pad. Then she sat back and smiled into the telephone.

"Don't worry, Mrs. Gray, we've covered every detail. Your daughter's wedding reception is going to be very special."

In a few moments, her mother had hung up. The smile drained from her face as she studied her own daughter. "So...what did the police have to say? And, what did you tell them?"

"You don't mean 'the police'. You mean Detective Thompson," Eliza corrected, buying time. She should have figured out before now what she would tell her mother.

Her mother frowned. "Eliza, quit stalling."

Thinking fast, Eliza said, "Detective Thompson asked me not to talk about this, but I'm sure he didn't mean to my own mother. Yesterday, I saw a man with his arms around a woman. They were in Fiona Dulaney's room and the man's back was to me."

Her mother's eyes widened. "Was the woman Fiona Dulaney?"

"I couldn't see much of her, just her reddish-blond hair."

"How about the man? Did you recognize him? Did you get

a good look at him?"

"No, Mom. It was kind of embarrassing, so I got out of there in a hurry."

Mary Lou, one of the sales representatives, stuck her head in the door. "Linda, do you want to talk to Steve Cassidy?"

"No—I mean, just ask him to wait a moment. We've been playing phone tag all morning," Eliza's mom said, glancing at Mary Lou for a split second before returning her attention to Eliza.

"I don't understand how you could have overseen a couple embracing in Fiona Dulaney's room..."

"The door was open, Mom," Eliza said, quelling a stab of guilt by reasoning that the door was, indeed, open when she saw the couple. She was only omitting the fact that she'd opened the door herself.

Marie, the most junior sales representative, entered the room with a timid glance at Linda. "I'm sorry to interrupt, but Mike in food and beverage is on line three. He wants to know whether it would be okay to set up the GE Fanuc conference room first thing in the morning rather than tonight."

Eliza's mother sighed impatiently. "Mike knows it needs to be set up tonight! The GE people need to get in there early. He and I have discussed this... Thank you, Marie. I'll talk to him."

Although Eliza knew that Steve Cassidy and Mike Gleason in food and beverage were saving her from answering lots of questions, she experienced a perverse resentment. She had wanted to see her mom, but, as usual, other people came first.

Her face must have revealed her unhappiness because her mother came around her desk and gave her a brief hug. "Sorry, sweetheart. We'll talk later."

As Eliza exited her mother's office, she knew chances were slim that her mother would quiz her again. She should have been relieved.

Eliza retraced her steps, heading down the corridor to the employee stairwell. As the heavy steel door of the stairwell banged shut behind her, she panicked. Whirling around, she yanked the door open and plunged back into the corridor. She would take the long route. The smell of dust and metal, the gray walls of the stairwell, the concrete stairs with their iron handrails, the glaring florescence and the tunnel-like confinement reminded Eliza of a prison. Worse than this was the knowledge that someone evil had visited the hotel last night. *He could still be here.*

Chapter 4

The young woman ran across an open field, her long hair a stream of reddish-gold in the moonlight. Her high heels caught on thick tussocks of grass and her long, silk dress hampered her stride. One foot landed in a hole hidden by the rough grass and she stumbled and fell, ripping the delicate fabric of her dress. Awkwardly, she thrust herself up off the ground and continued her flight.

At first, Eliza watched the unfolding drama with distant concern, until, to her horror, she herself was running across the dark landscape. She had become the fleeing woman. When she reached the edge of the field, she gazed up and down the road in a panic before noticing a lighted dwelling set well back in the woods across the road. At first the house was a distant beacon of safety and hope, but as she drew closer, a sense of foreboding settled upon her, slowing her footsteps.

As she turned back toward the main road, a shadowy figure stepped out of the darkness and whispered, "E-li-za." There was something familiar about the figure if she could just think, but Eliza's mind was frozen with terror. She opened her mouth to scream. All that came out was a choked gasp, but it was enough to wake her from the nightmare. She lay still for several moments, heart hammering against her chest.

Eliza glanced at her bedside clock and, seeing that it was almost 7:00 a.m., switched off the alarm. She lay there getting her bearings. It was Monday. She had spent most of Sunday at the public library researching a term paper. The events of the last two days had surfaced in her mind several times but were pushed aside so that she could continue her research. Obviously, thoughts of the murder, so firmly banished during the day, had returned last night with double force to haunt her dreams.

Forcing herself to move, Eliza rolled out of bed and headed for the bathroom. While she was showering, dressing and blow-drying her hair, the dream haunted her thoughts. The fleeing woman at the nightmare's beginning reminded her of Fiona. She had traded places with a dead woman, a murder victim. A shiver went down her spine.

An hour later when Eliza arrived at school, she was still mired in the dark mood of her dream. As she shuffled along behind the stream of students pouring into the school, someone fell into step beside her. She glanced at him in wary surprise, before recognizing him. He was one of the McClellans, the people who owned the farm where she and her mother lived. She knew he attended Albemarle High School, but he was a year or two ahead of her.

"Hello, Eliza," he said, a smile lighting his nice, regular features. "Seeing that we're neighbors, I should have introduced myself before. I'm Joe McClellan."

Eliza smiled, tentatively. "Good to meet you, Joe."

A flicker of embarrassment crossed Joe's face. "I've got kind of selfish reasons for introducing myself today."

Eliza waited a few beats for him to continue, shooting small sideways glances at this affable stranger in faded jeans and plaid flannel shirt who was only half a head taller than she. The awkwardness she felt walking beside him was somewhat alleviated by her curiosity about what he was going to say next.

As they were passing an empty classroom, Joe came to a halt. "Look, could we stop for a moment and talk?"

Eliza nodded and followed him into the classroom.

Joe helped her unload her backpack onto the first desk they came to. He placed his hands on the back of the desk and their eyes met.

His eyes were large with thick, sooty lashes and irises that reminded her of the depths of the Atlantic Ocean, an alive and intense gray-blue. Now that he had her undivided attention, he began to speak. "You know about the Crime Busters Club, don't you?"

Eliza nodded. It was an Albemarle High School club that studied local crime on a case-by-case basis—sometimes attempting to solve the crime and other times just following the actions of law enforcement. When she first heard about the club, she was eager to join. Then she showed up late for the first meeting, and, after a quick glance around the room, she made a hasty exit. The group was small, and every member defined the word 'nerd'. Joe must have missed that meeting. She tuned back into what he was saying.

"We're starting a new column in the school newspaper called 'Sleuth'. It's based on whatever crime the club is following. I'm going to delay the first 'Sleuth' article until I have something really intriguing—something that will generate more interest in the club. The murder at the Silver Fox Inn would be perfect, a real attention-grabber. Unfortunately, the police haven't released much information. Since your mom works there, I was hoping you could help me out. Even a few extra details would be great."

Eliza glanced away, staring out the window at the inner courtyard where sidewalks crisscrossed red-brown dirt and clumps of faded grass in an attempt to connect the various wings of the sprawling school. Although her eyes were focused on the courtyard, her mind was centered on those brief moments when she opened the door to Room 123 and saw the entwined couple. *If only Joe knew what details I could furnish*, she thought to herself. *It would make a great news story. The headline would read 'Possible eyewitness to killer's embrace.'*

Eliza returned her gaze to Joe. "There's really nothing I can tell you that wasn't in the newspaper."

Joe's face fell into lines of disappointment. "When you took so long to answer, I was sure you had something to say."

"Sorry, Joe." Eliza grabbed a shoulder strap on her backpack.

His fingers closed around her arm and she froze, looking at him half in question and half in protest.

Joe released her, instantly. "I know there's something you could tell me... Why can't you talk? Are you afraid?"

Eliza shook her head. "It's not that. I was interviewed by the police, along with the hotel staff. Detective Thompson, the man in charge, warned me to keep my mouth shut."

Joe's gray-blue gaze was steady and sincere. "Look, the last thing I'd want to do is get you in trouble. End of inquisition." He smiled ruefully. "This murder has me really curious and it would be perfect for Sleuth, but I'll back off. Promise me you won't run in the opposite direction the next time you see me coming."

She smiled at the image this invoked. "I promise."

Eliza slung her backpack over one shoulder and strode swiftly to the door, resisting the impulse to glance back. She headed for her locker, the smile still hovering around the corners of her mouth, hardly noticing the students swarming about her. As she approached her locker, she saw Sydney waiting there.

Sydney's face lit up with her trademark sweet, pearly-toothed smile. "Hey, Eliza. Where've you been?"

"Hey," Eliza said, smiling back. As she shoved books in her locker, she made a quick decision not to mention Joe. She told herself it was because she didn't want to discuss the murder.

"The bus was late, the halls are crammed..."

"Well, let's not stand around talkin'," Sydney interrupted. "The gang's waitin' for us."

Waiting for you maybe, Eliza thought to herself, but she accompanied her friend. They threaded their way through the crowds, until they reached a little-used side door leading to a small concrete pad where three girls stood smoking.

A tall girl with trendy, severely short hair and a close-cut, black leather jacket glanced over Eliza's head at Sydney. "Well, look who finally showed up. The bell's going to ring any minute."

Sydney draped one arm over the tall girl's shoulders. "Diana, where's the fire? We're here aren't we?"

Diana managed a smile. "Yeah, you're here. Would you like a smoke?"

As Sydney helped herself to Diana's pack, Diana looked at Eliza, finally acknowledging her existence. "How about you? Care for a cigarette?"

Eliza stared up at the taller girl's face, trying to decide whether it was Diana's heavily outlined raccoon eyes or her dark-purple lipstick that made her face look so hard. She had turned down Diana's repeated offers for a cigarette ever since Sydney introduced them a few months ago. Now, Eliza wanted desperately to shock Diana—to seize her by the lapels of her shiny-black jacket and shake some respect out of her.

"Sure, I'd love one." Eliza took the packet from Sydney's hand. All four girls stared as she put a cigarette in her mouth.

"Well, doesn't anybody have a light?"

As Sydney held up a lighted match, Eliza breathed in, concentrating on not revealing her distaste for the bitter tobacco flavor.

At first Diana looked non-plussed, then she noticed the way

Eliza held the cigarette between her thumb and first finger. She snickered, catching the eye of a pale, plump girl named Amanda so that she joined in.

Eliza laughed too, choking on the smoke. She must have looked absurd, affecting to know what she was doing with a cigarette. Kristen, a pretty, curly-haired brunette with a bizarre laugh, cackled like a witch. Now, everyone was laughing. As Eliza chuckled and coughed, eyes watering, Diana shot her a look of approval. Eliza was amazed.

The bell rang with its usual tyrannical din.

"Hey, Eliza, I'll meet you outside the cafeteria at lunch," said Sydney.

"Sounds good," Eliza responded.

She chucked the cigarette onto the concrete and ground out the flame with the toe of her boot until the cigarette butt resembled a squashed insect. If only it were as easy to grind out the first faint feelings of self-disgust creeping into her system like a slow poison.

Chapter 5

Eliza entered the hotel that afternoon full of determination. She pulled out the pocket notebook she had purchased at the school supply store and checked to see whether her pen was still securely clipped to the spirals. She could make notes whenever necessary, plus she could be relatively unobtrusive.

As she walked through the hotel lobby, she passed Campbell pushing a luggage rack piled high with suitcases, boxes and garment bags. He smiled, his face glowing even more than usual with a fine layer of perspiration. The hotel was waking up from its long winter freeze, and Campbell seemed to share Eliza's delight. In a month or two, the place would be a whirl of activity with the guest rooms, conference rooms and restaurants bursting at the seams.

"Lots of homework?" her mother inquired.

Eliza jumped then turned around. Her mother had appeared out of nowhere.

"Actually, it's not bad today," Eliza admitted.

"Great. Well, as you can see, things are beginning to pick up here. I'll see you later, sweetie." Her mother gave her a light, perfumed hug and strode swiftly across the carpet to the waiting elevator, disappearing with a lipsticked smile and an elegant wave.

Eliza headed for the employee conference room. She liked this arrangement. The cottage where she and her mother lived was an empty and isolated place to go after school. Eliza's mother had asked Mr. Austen, the general manager, if Eliza could study at the inn. When first approached about the idea, Mr. Austen was amenable on a trial basis. After all, Linda Derby, the hotel sales director, was one of his most valuable employees. Almost one year later, there had been no negative repercussions and Eliza was an established presence at the inn.

She dropped her backpack on the small conference table with a thud. Ignoring the door that led to the lobby, Eliza opened the door on the opposite end of the room. She was now in the long, narrow front desk area, but not the windowed portion where she would have been visible to guests.

The switchboard hummed softly and a smooth, self-important voice said, "Good afternoon, the Silver Fox Inn, Johnny speaking."

Eliza recognized the stiff navy-jacketed shoulders and the pompous tones of Johnny Burnett, the desk clerk seated at the console. Several feet beyond Johnny stood Jordan Blake in the straight, hands-clasped-behind-the-back posture the clerks had been taught to adopt when standing in the windowed portion of the desk. Eliza waved to Jordan. He wiggled his fingers back in a fashion guaranteed to look ridiculous with his formal stance and the solemn expression he wore on his handsome, dark features.

Eliza giggled as she thrust open the heavy door onto the hallway leading to the kitchen, the food and beverage office and housekeeping. When she entered the kitchen, the aroma of bread baking drew her attention until someone knocked into a tall stack of plastic trays. The trays wavered back and forth, then fell in an earsplitting cascade. There was only a slight and momentary reduction in the normal kitchen racket while people in the immediate vicinity stopped their activities and looked around to see what had happened.

Eliza sidestepped the fallen trays and caught the eye of the pastry chef, Colin Gentry, a new staff member and friend, only a few years older than she. He pointed at a tray of delectables in front of him. His expressive brown eyes and handsome, strong-boned face asked, *Do you want any?* Seconds later, Eliza was at Colin's side, eyes closing as a spoonful of his silky-smooth, velvety-soft 'Sunburst' flan dissolved on her tongue like manna from heaven. The scent of freshly peeled oranges filled her nostrils, briefly transporting her to some warm, sun-filled place.

"Ah, Eliza. Clearly, the way to your heart is through your sweet tooth. Pretty soon you'll be hooked on me," Colin said with an exaggerated leer.

Eliza wrinkled her nose. "Sorry to disappoint you, but I'm hooked on your desserts, not on you."

Colin feigned disappointment, but Eliza knew that she could pay him no higher compliment. He grinned broadly as she popped a puff pastry into her mouth. Thanking her lucky stars for an overactive metabolism, she strolled over to the soft drink dispenser. For someone with a queen-sized sweet tooth, having access to the inn's unending supply of luscious desserts was a monumental perk. Dusting off her fingers, she filled a tall glass with Dr. Pepper.

Back in the employee conference room, Eliza rapidly completed a math handout and a grammar exercise. She brushed off the navy blazer she'd draped over the back of her chair and slipped it on. Then, she opened a closet and peered into a narrow, full-length mirror attached to the back of the door. For the umpteenth time, she wished for a small, pretty nose rather than one that was a tad too long and pointy. Then, pushing the useless thought away, she pulled a brush through her unruly hair until she was presentable.

As the child of an inn employee, she needed to dress

appropriately at all times. Her mother had given in, finally, and let her wear well-pressed, 'classic-cut' jeans without any holes. After all, it was practical during those brisk afternoon walks to the inn or if she wanted to go riding. Her mother compensated for the jeans by supplying Eliza with several blazers and a slew of designer and hand-knit sweaters.

Usually, a long day at school followed by homework left her feeling sluggish. This afternoon, her mind was clear and alert; her body pumped with energy and purpose. She would find out all she could about Fiona Dulaney's murder, starting with the hotel department in which she was most at home, the front desk.

When she entered the narrow, cave-like space, Jordan and Johnny had switched places so that Jordan was on the switchboard and Johnny was checking in someone at the front desk. To Eliza's delight, Devin Cooper was standing near Johnny. The beautiful strawberry-blond was giving directions to a gray-haired couple, a large man with a permanent frown and his wisp of a self-effacing wife. Devin's clear, distinctive voice was easily discernible from where Eliza stood.

"Drive past the main building to the lodging wing of the hotel on your right. Once you enter the building, turn right and your room will be on your left about half way down. Would you like any assistance with your luggage?"

The husband shook his head, curtly. "We can manage. But there is one thing. We were guaranteed a lake-view room."

"You've been assigned a lake-view room," Devin said. "Just for future reference, we can never make guarantees, but we try very hard to honor requests. As you can see, we have an excellent track record." Devin smiled.

Her smile lit up her lovely features and Eliza could see the ire melting away from the naturally bellicose husband's face.

Instead of blustering some more, he thanked Devin and escorted his wife from the lobby.

Meanwhile, a conservatively dressed, middle-aged woman approached the front desk. Johnny had finished up with his previous guests.

"Checking in?" Johnny inquired.

"Yes. The reservation is under 'Sara Mascara'," the woman replied.

Johnny pulled the reservation form from the file and placed it on the counter. "Miss Mascara, please sign here," he said in his distant, condescending voice as he marked the signature line with a pen.

Devin had left the windowed portion of the desk in order to freshen her lipstick. When Sara Mascara departed, Devin looked up from her mirrored compact and smiled teasingly at Jordan. "There goes your chance to meet the lovely Miss Mascara."

Jordan shook his head in mock misery. "Alas. My fantasies of a long-lashed cover girl were bound to be disappointed. Besides, I did register James Bond the other evening."

"No way!" Eliza protested, figuring that Jordan was joking. "Nobody has parents that cruel."

Jordan nodded his head. "'Fraid so. The guy wasn't bad looking either. Tall executive-type. There was only one catch. He was as bald as they come."

"Did you give him the VIP treatment?" Devin asked.

Jordan stood up. His teeth gleamed in a wide smile and he bowed slightly, welcoming an imaginary presence. "Bond? James Bond?"

He flipped through an invisible reservations file and withdrew James Bond's reservation. His movements held a cat-like grace and precision, and Eliza watched in fascination, knowing Devin was doing the same.

"Sign here, Mr. Bond. I see you flew in from Atlanta, Mr. Bond. How was your flight, Mr. Bond? Will you need assistance with your luggage, Mr. Bond? Shall I arrange for a wake up call, Mr. Bond?"

Jordan's British accent was flawless, his demeanor polished yet respectful. One moment he was facing 'James Bond' and the next he was grinning wickedly at Eliza and Devin—gold-flecked, hazel eyes glittering.

Devin shook her head. "You didn't use a British accent did you, Jordan?"

Jordan raised a quizzical eyebrow, a regular feat of his that Eliza had tried hard to imitate. "Why, yes. It was frightfully brilliant," he stated in his posh accent. Then, as Johnny joined them, "What do you say, old bean?"

Johnny's thin lips tightened. "I wouldn't call it 'brilliant'. You're just lucky Mr. Bond thought you were British—so he didn't take offense."

Eliza swallowed a giggle. Here's Jordan being outrageously funny and Johnny probably didn't even laugh. He was just relieved that the guest didn't catch on.

Devin laughed. "Oh, Johnny. The whole thing was wasted on you. I wish I'd been there!"

Johnny, who was usually as expressionless as Mattel's Ken doll, actually flinched. He began massaging his neck, a habit whenever he was uncomfortable. Jordan claimed that this mannerism was caused by the constriction of Johnny's starchy collars.

Devin grasped one of Johnny's biceps and squeezed. "I'm sorry. A lot of really masculine men don't seem to have a sense of humor. I guess a lot of the time they're shouldering serious burdens so it's hard for them to loosen up."

As the hurt melted from Johnny's face, Jordan caught Eliza's eye and winked. Eliza ignored him. She knew that Jordan found Devin manipulative. But Eliza thought Devin was just a natural-born actress who wanted to be liked and didn't want to hurt people's feelings. After all, Devin had gone out of her way to be nice to Eliza, even though Eliza was several years younger. She couldn't help it if guys like Johnny hung onto her every word and gesture.

"Excuse me." A dry-as-dust, male voice interrupted Eliza's thoughts.

All three clerks moved automatically toward the voice. From where she stood, well away from the front desk window, Eliza could see the clerks, but the guest with the dry voice was out of her field of vision.

"May I help you?" Johnny asked.

"This is most annoying," said the guest.

Johnny waited a few beats. "What's annoying, sir?"

"I can't seem to find my room," the voice rasped querulously.

Johnny's wooden features managed to arrange themselves into an expression of patronizing contempt.

Before Johnny could respond, Jordan stepped forward. "Forgive me for interrupting, but I checked you in, sir. Henry Durrer—isn't that right?"

"Yes. Could you direct me to my room, young man?" the old gentleman said, his voice regaining some dignity.

"Just give me a moment, Mr. Durrer, and I'll be happy to escort you," Jordan said. If the old man had been surrounded by advisers and security guards and Mr. Durrer had been called 'Mr. President', Jordan's manner and tone would have been perfectly fitting.

While Jordan looked up Mr. Durrer's room number and grabbed the key, Johnny stepped away from the window and stage-whispered something about 'blue-heads' to Devin. Eliza stiffened, hoping the old man was hard of hearing. She'd heard remarks about 'blue heads' before. The arrival of a senior citizen bus tour sometimes triggered the rude announcement—'Here come the blue-heads'—referring to the rinse used to brighten gray hair.

Then Eliza made out the word 'Alzheimer's' in Devin's whispered response. Johnny snickered and Eliza thought that this was the first time she'd heard Johnny laugh—if something so mean and furtive could be called laughter.

She was relieved to see Jordan heading out to the lobby. Now, she wouldn't worry about what the old man overheard. She settled down at a desk in the far corner of the front desk area, resting her chin on her palm to think. How was she going to bring up the murder? She discarded one conversational gambit after the next until Jordan returned several minutes later. Then she followed him over to the others and plunged right in.

"I keep wishing that somehow I could have prevented Fiona Dulaney's murder," she said. Everyone stared at her with puzzled expressions and she hastened to clarify her statement. "I mean, I was right here at the hotel and, if I'd only known what was going on, maybe there was something I could have done."

Eliza's voice tightened as she uttered the last few words. The others had no way of knowing how close she had probably come to interrupting the murder. For the hundredth time she recalled the flash of time when she had stood in the doorway of Room 123. Had she missed some vital clue as to whether the man was embracing Fiona Dulaney or squeezing the life from her? Had she seen any detail that could point to his identity?

Jordan laid an arm across her shoulders. "Come on, sweetheart. You look so sad and positively guilt-stricken. Are you supposed to be clairvoyant?"

Eliza shook her head. "Do you guys find yourselves thinking about what you were doing when the murder was taking place?" She gazed carefully into their faces, gauging their reactions.

Devin smiled sadly. "I have thought about it, more than once. I was over a hundred miles from here at a lovely bed and breakfast when poor Fiona lost her life."

Jordan shrugged, a look of chagrin stealing across his features. "I spent most of my time at the library cramming for an exam yesterday afternoon and evening."

Eliza knew that, as a University of Virginia senior double majoring in economics and drama on a scholarship, Jordan was usually either working to pay for his room and board or studying at the library. As he'd once explained, his cramped and overcrowded apartment was not ideal for studying. Thinking about her own recent stint at the public library, Eliza felt sorry for him. She tuned back into what Jordan was saying.

"Guess this makes me insensitive, but I hadn't thought about it in relation to Fiona Dulaney. What about you, Johnny?"

Johnny's hand returned to his throat. "No, I hadn't given it any thought, either," he said, pronouncing the 'ei' in 'either' as if it were a long i. "Let's see, what was I doing? Yesterday afternoon I purchased new tires for my Saab over at Sears and was forced to wait for ages. Sears had a big automotive sale and the place was an absolute zoo. It was pitch dark by the time I left."

Jordan raised an eyebrow. "Why, Johnny, what were you and the 'Snaab' doing slumming at Sears? I thought you took the Snaab to the luxury car dealership where you purchased her."

Eliza bit her lip to keep from smiling. She was concentrating so hard on the conversation that she jumped when a tall, amply proportioned woman stuck her head through the front desk window. "I need a couple of strong men to help me carry some boxes into my office and the bellmen are all busy."

Katie Wood, the marketing director, never asked for favors unless it was necessary. She had a strong maternal streak and was a phenomenal cook, often bringing them homemade bread, cookies and cakes. Jordan leapt to her assistance, disappearing before a scowling Johnny even took his first, stiff-legged step forward. Eliza had noticed before how much Johnny resented any task that might be described as menial.

While Johnny was aggravated by Katie's interruption, Eliza was pleased. She had established where her friends were at the time of the murder. Now she had an opportunity to have a one-on-one talk with Devin about the murder victim. "Devin, you and Fiona Dulaney were close, weren't you?"

Devin nodded. "We were assigned to share a dormitory room during our first year at Sweet Briar College. After that, we made arrangements to be roommates every year."

"What was she like?"

"Everyone wanted to be Fiona's friend. She was funny and smart, always laughing. She never had to try very hard. Her father paid for the best of everything."

Eliza wondered whether she was imagining Devin's slightly derisive undertone. Surely, Devin, recovering from the shock and sadness of Fiona's death, would not be critical of her. "Was Fiona's family extremely wealthy?"

Devin smiled. "Have you ever heard of Dulaney's Fine Spices?'"

"Oh." Eliza pictured the spices in her mother's pantry. Dulaney's was practically a household name among those who were, or aspired to be, gourmet chefs. Cheeks flaming, she plowed ahead. "Fiona sounds very social. Was she into school at all?"

"Oh, Fiona was exceptionally intelligent. Plus, she had a great background—the best schools, tutors, foreign travel..."

"What did Fiona do after college?" Eliza asked.

"She was always involved in art and design at school," Devin said, unclasping a bracelet and handing it to Eliza. "She made that for me when we were at college. After college, her father helped her get started in the jewelry business. She had a boutique in Washington, DC, where she sold her own work and the work of other artists."

Eliza was studying the bracelet. It was a wide bangle of burnished gold molded in a freeform shape with a zigzag pattern flowing across the surface. A small gem hovered in the middle like the sun rising over jagged mountains. As Eliza turned the bracelet in her hands, the gem caught the feeble overhead light and sent it shimmering in different directions. "Wow! Is this a real diamond?"

Devin shrugged. "Fiona worked with only the finest stones and pearls. It was a point of contention with her father. He thought the store would make more of a profit if Fiona didn't limit herself to such expensive materials."

Eliza decided she'd better cut to the chase. Jordan and Johnny would be back soon. "Did Fiona have any enemies?"

Devin shook her head. "Not that I know of. Like I said, she had a carefree attitude that was contagious. People liked her; they liked to be around her."

"Why would anyone kill her?" Eliza speculated aloud.

"It seems pretty clear to me," Devin said.

Eliza looked at her in surprise.

"He was after her gems," Devin stated, calmly.

"How do you know there were gems in her room?" Eliza asked. Guests were encouraged to store valuables in the hotel vault.

Devin was silent for a moment and this time when she spoke there was no missing the cutting quality to her voice. "She was quite reckless in that regard. She liked to have her stuff with her. Jewels were her toys."

Chapter 6

The next morning Eliza's mother had a breakfast meeting in town, so she dropped Eliza off at school. It was early, barely eight o'clock. Eliza's body was on automatic pilot, her brain in a fog. As she strode down the corridor, someone called her name and it took her several seconds to respond. Finally, she looked around and there was Joe McClellan, practically at her elbow.

His hair was neatly combed and damp and he was wearing another plaid flannel shirt and freshly laundered jeans. "I thought you promised not to run in the opposite direction when you saw me coming," he said, puffing slightly.

"I wasn't running," Eliza pointed out.

"Well you sure do walk fast for someone your size."

Eliza frowned. "Watch yourself, buster."

"Hey, sorry," Joe said. "I'm not exactly a basketball player myself."

"No. You get your exercise chasing people down," Eliza responded, then winced inwardly. Where had that come from? She didn't usually make cracks at people.

Joe was unfazed. "Touché. Now we're even," he said.

"You wanna know if I've changed my mind about discussing the murder. Am I right?" Eliza snapped.

"No. I mean—there's nothing I'd like better than your input on the murder, but that's not why I was 'chasing you down'," Joe said, firmly.

They'd reached her locker and, swinging her heavy backpack

to the floor, she began dialing the combination.

Joe reached out and placed his hand over hers on the dial, sending a tingle of surprised awareness up her arm. She jerked her hand away and spun toward him.

"I was wondering whether you'd like to go horseback riding with me after school," he said quietly, as if calming a skittish filly. "I've often seen you riding along the road near the Silver Fox Inn and thought about asking you to ride with me at the farm. Today is supposed to reach fifty degrees for the first time since early December."

Now, Eliza felt badly about misreading his motivations. She met his direct, intense, gray-blue gaze and was briefly immobilized. Blinking, she forced herself to think about the question at hand. There were some beautiful trails on the McClellan farm, and she had only just begun to explore them on foot.

"I'd love to go riding," she responded.

Joe grinned, revealing a deep cleft in his left cheek. "Great! I'll meet you at the barn around four o'clock."

"All right," she said, coolly.

Eliza watched Joe stride away so confident and sure. She knew he drove to school everyday in a rusty and dented pickup. Why hadn't he offered to drive her home? On the other hand, driving with friends entailed the third degree from her mother. Maybe Joe had even given that some thought and was just being considerate. Now all she had to do was leave a message explaining her plans with the sales office receptionist.

Seven hours later, Eliza found herself astride a small chestnut mare. Dancer was as smooth and graceful as her name implied with manners to match. Joe switched from a trot to a canter and Eliza sat deep in the saddle and tightened her right rein while squeezing her right leg against Dancer's side. Dancer broke into a canter, and, as the trail was wide at this point, Eliza dug in her legs and leaned forward. The little mare flew past Joe and his mount, a big gray gelding called Sterling Silver, taking them by surprise.

It wasn't until they'd cleared the woods that Eliza heard the gelding's hoofbeats gaining ground. Within a minute, Joe and Sterling were neck and neck.

Joe's teeth flashed in a wide smile. "Race you to the big oak tree!"

Eliza spotted a mammoth oak half a mile away, standing by itself on the top of a hill. Seconds later Joe and the big gray broke free, thundering along the fence line toward a creek that divided them from their target. Eliza and Dancer galloped after them until Eliza spotted a chickencoop jump built right into the fence line in typical hunt-country fashion. Did she dare?

The chickencoop wasn't that large, and Eliza couldn't resist. She veered Dancer away from the fence in order to allow for an easy approach to the chickencoop. Dancer longed to race after the gelding, but she was too well trained to put up a serious resistance. When she spotted the chickencoop her ears pricked. They soared into the air effortlessly, Eliza leaning forward in perfect synchrony with the mare's athletic leap.

Now, Eliza and Dancer had shaved off half the distance required to reach the oak and they galloped triumphantly toward the tree. They pulled up beneath its bare, dark branches and watched the competition approach them at a leisurely canter, now that the race was at an end. Eliza admired the picture Joe made sitting straight yet relaxed in the saddle.

Joe pulled the gelding up in front of Eliza and Dancer, grinning widely, that deep dimple flashing in his left cheek. "You've bested me and on my own land, too!"

Eliza smiled back, partially in relief. "I hope it was all right to jump her. That chickencoop was just beckoning to us and Dancer took it like it was a foot high."

Joe's gaze was as direct as ever. "I would have been annoyed if you hadn't negotiated the jump so smoothly, but, truthfully, in your shoes, I would have done the same thing myself. You're quite the rider, Eliza."

She felt her cheeks growing warm. "Thanks. You're not bad yourself."

Eliza looked away toward the sweeping view ahead of them, breathing in great draughts of crisp, clean air spiced by the musky scent of warm horseflesh. Even leached of color—the rolling fields, the white-mottled Sycamores, the stand of tall pines, the meandering creek and the hazy, blue mountains beyond fed an inner longing for beauty lodged deep within her. Judging by his silence and the peaceful expression on his face, Joe felt the same.

"Makes you feel like writing poetry," Eliza said.

Joe's eyebrows rose in surprise. "Do you like to write?"

"Yes," Eliza said. "But I haven't done much. Besides school assignments, I've entered a few story-writing and essay contests, that's all."

"Bring some of your stuff to school tomorrow. I'd love to read it—if you don't mind?" Joe requested, tagging on the question as an obvious afterthought.

"Sure," Eliza said. It was the least she could do after he had provided her with such a lovely afternoon.

"You should consider writing for the school newspaper," Joe went on, eagerly. "We've got a terrific staff, and, if you ever wanted to write professionally, it's a great background to have."

"You're right. But I've given it some serious thought in the past and kept coming to the same conclusion. I'm just not ready for that kind of time commitment," Eliza said, shying away from Joe's enthusiasm.

Her mind flashed to the first time she'd spotted Joe at school, just outside the newspaper office. Even from a distance, he stood out as being the leader of the small group standing around him in a rough circle. Eliza remembered a boy built like a beanpole with Eddie Fisher glasses; a short, heavy-set boy with an earnest, pink-skinned face and a tall girl whose serious expression and armload of books spoiled her handsome good looks. If she remembered correctly, a couple of these same people had been at the Crime Busters club meeting. They'd certainly fit right in.

Eliza shook off the memory, focusing on her surroundings once more. "From here, it seems like we're deep in the country. I just see a couple of homes and the rest is land. It gives you a feeling of space and freedom."

Joe nodded. "Yeah, I know what you mean. There's a lot less open land around here than there used to be, though. My dad and mom love to talk about how when they were kids they used to ride for miles over farms and rough countryside, fox hunting. Now, a lot of the farms and the wild and empty spaces have been taken over by residential developers. Charlottesville is growing and people love these mountain views."

Eliza noticed a big white, columned house in the distance. "Who lives in the 'Gone With the Wind' house over there?"

Joe smiled and shook his head. "Sometimes I forget that you've lived in Charlottesville only a short time. Everybody around here knows that's the Dulaney place."

"Dulaney, as in *Fiona* Dulaney?" Eliza asked in surprise.

"You've got it," Joe said. "Her parents used to live there before they moved away. Now Paul Dulaney's sister, Susan

Burnett, lives there with her son. The place has really gone downhill."

"If the Dulaney's are so wealthy, why doesn't Mr. Dulaney's sister take care of the place?" Eliza wondered aloud.

"Paul Dulaney started out with a decent amount of money and made a lot more. His sister probably had the same to start with, but she married a guy with a drug addiction. Their life together was a downward spiral and her husband died a few years ago," Joe explained.

Eliza felt a faint stirring of her memory, but before she could grasp its significance a gust of wind rattled the oak tree branches sending Joe's gelding skittering sideways. The sky was darkening and the slight breeze present during the beginning of their ride had become a chill wind. Simultaneously, she and Joe turned their horses in the direction of the stable. The mare and gelding trotted eagerly toward their warm stalls and buckets of feed.

A few hours later when Eliza was lying in bed, she thought about the time she had spent horseback riding with Joe. She couldn't remember a more wonderful afternoon. Dancer and she had been perfectly matched. She was flattered that Joe had let her ride such a valuable animal. Her regular mount from the Silver Fox Inn's stable was a sweet old guy, but at almost 17 hands he was rather large for her and, compared to Dancer, his gaits were clumsy and rough.

Eliza shifted the pillow beneath her head and admitted to herself that Dancer was not the only reason she had enjoyed herself that afternoon. Joe's character was composed of a unique blend of qualities that somehow put her at ease. He was upbeat and self-assured, not needing to prove his masculinity. She thought about how that morning he had taken her wisecracks about his height and journalistic snooping in stride. Then, that afternoon he had enjoyed the race she initiated, caring not a whit that he and his mount had been bested.

As Eliza's mind circled round and round the afternoon with Joe, it replayed their conversation about the Dulaney Place. Again, Eliza felt a faint stirring in her memory, as if an elusive, but familiar ghost drifted there momentarily, disappearing before she could identify it.

Chapter 7

Eliza slid across the school bus seat and a chubby boy, a freshman she didn't know, sat down heavily in the spot she'd just vacated. He coughed with a deep, rattling gusto, causing Eliza to scoot over even further until her hip and shoulder were touching the metal wall of the bus. The boy pulled a laptop computer from his backpack and settled it upon his plump thighs. Eliza shook her head. After a long day at school, he couldn't wait to fire up his computer? *What a technogeek*, she thought.

Then Eliza had to smile as she reached into her jeans pocket for the tiny notebook representative of her own obsession. Take away his cough and his bulk and this boy was the perfect companion for someone who preferred a quiet bus ride home. She turned to a fresh page and wrote 'To Do' at the top. Scanning her notes, she was reminded that Fiona was dining with a 'Brad Pitt' look-alike the day she was murdered. Eliza jotted, '(l) Find Brad Pitt guy.' *How? Someone must have recognized him.* Then she wrote, '(2) Question Brad Pitt. Did Fiona tell him she was meeting someone after lunch?' Of course, the Brad Pitt look-alike could be the killer, making that question irrelevant.

Eliza chewed on her pen, thinking. If she had interrupted Fiona's killer—then most likely Fiona died shortly afterwards. The plan was to meet Sydney for Pay Per View around 4:45 p.m. Her watch had read 4:30 p.m. when she left the front desk. How long would it take her to get to Room 123? Five, ten minutes? Eliza removed the pen from her mouth and scribbled, '(3) Time walk between front desk & Room 123.'

When did Fiona hook up with the killer? Someone must have seen her between two o'clock-ish when she finished lunch and four-forty-ish. Eliza wrote, '(4) Check reservations book & wait staff re when Fiona arrived and departed. Check w/ wait staff re Brad Pitt's identity. (5) Check w/ hotel staff re whether anyone saw Fiona after she left restaurant.' Eliza thought some more, gazing at her list now and again.

The computer nerd blew his nose gustily and Eliza leaned as far away from him as possible into the window. As she stared through the glass, she was amazed to see the Silver Fox Inn sign just ahead. The half-hour drive had seemed to take mere minutes. She shoved her notebook and pen back into her pocket, zipped up her parka, threw her backpack over one shoulder and hurried off the bus.

Although the inn driveway was only about three-quarters of a mile in length, Eliza wished she could fly the distance. The wind whipped about her, and she lengthened her stride, tucking her hair into the neck of her jacket and pulling on a pair of leather, cashmere-lined riding gloves. By the time she arrived at the glass double doors, her eyes were watering and her nose felt like an icicle.

Campbell held one door open wide, his glowing face and warm smile as welcome as the heated air that enveloped her. "Good afternoon, young lady."

Eliza's frozen skin and dry lips tightened as she smiled in return. "Hi, Campbell. How's it going?"

He glanced behind him at the empty lobby. "A little quiet for my taste."

She nodded. "I know what you mean."

Campbell pulled a cloth from his pocket and wiped a microscopic speck of dirt from the glass. "It'll pick up tomorrow. Big conference this weekend."

She smiled wider this time, her face beginning to thaw. "Good!"

It was time to check in with her mother then tackle her homework. She strode off toward the 'back of the house,' as they say in the hotel trade, pushing through a door that read 'Employees Only'.

Two hours later, Eliza slammed her trigonometry book shut. *Done!* She slipped on the tweed blazer draped over the back of her chair and consulted the closet mirror. Same old pointy nose, but the blazer's heathery blues and purples complemented her large, indigo eyes, the one physical attribute of which she was proud. Her hair, on the other hand, looked like she'd been in a pillow fight. Cursing its silky texture and sheer abundance, she brushed her hair impatiently and refastened her hair clip which had started the day at the crown of her head and had slipped down past her left ear. Now, her appearance was satisfactory.

Without having to consult her 'To Do' list, Eliza re-entered the 'front of the house' and headed toward the inn's main restaurant, hoping the volatile maitre d' hotel had the evening off. She spotted the maitre d's assistant standing near the restaurant entryway. Brian Hardwicke in a tuxedo was a formidably handsome young man, but Eliza was not intimidated. A new representative was needed in the sales department, and Brian had just submitted a resume. Eliza was confident that he would accommodate the sales director's daughter.

"Hi, Brian," Eliza said.

Brian smiled pleasantly. "Hello, Eliza. May I help you?"

"Were you here last Friday during lunch?" Eliza asked.

Brian gave her a puzzled look. "Yeah."

"Do you recall Fiona Dulaney having lunch that day?"

"Sure I do," Brian said. "She's a regular guest—I mean, she was a regular guest at the inn..."

"Do you remember the guy she was with?" Eliza asked eagerly.

Brian shot her another puzzled look, but he nodded. "He was tall, reminded me of some actor—"

"Do you know the man's name?" Eliza interrupted.

Brian looked confused. "The actor's name?"

Eliza shook her head impatiently. "No. The guy's real name."

"Sorry, I'd never seen him before," Brian said.

Eliza quelled her disappointment. "Could I see the reservation book?"

Brian walked behind the small desk placed just inside the doorway, flipped some pages and slid the open book across the desk's polished surface. "I can save you some time. The reservation was for one o'clock, and Miss Dulaney and her friend were here about an hour."

Eliza scanned the page headed Friday, February 26. Sure enough, 'Dulaney' was penciled in at one o'clock. If only the reservation had been made in her companion's name instead of hers. "How do you know how long Fiona stayed?"

"She was seated at one of our best, garden-view tables. Believe me, I keep track of those tables," Brian stated emphatically.

Eliza could see that he was growing annoyed. "You've been so helpful. I really appreciate it."

As if on cue, the telephone rang and Eliza slid the reservations book back across the desk. Brian flipped the pages forward, fielded questions about the restaurant's menu and price range, jotted down the last name and the size of the caller's party and repeated the reservation back to the caller, carefully.

Eliza listened to Brian with one corner of her mind, while

she realized she had not finished questioning him after all. As soon as he hung up, she was ready.

"Sorry, I thought of something else. Who else was working in the restaurant that day besides you and Maureen?"

"That's easy," Brian said. "We were short-staffed that day; only two people on the floor. Maureen was run off her feet. Tommy was working, too, but he'd just moved up from bus boy, and he was deadly slow."

"Is Tommy here today?"

Brian shook his head. "He worked breakfast and lunch, so he's probably long gone... You could ask Barry with the set-up crew. He and Tommy are friends—went to high school together or something. Sometimes they car pool."

"Thanks," Eliza said. "You've been a big help."

"Why are you so curious about last Friday?" Brian asked. Then it must have hit him. "Wait a minute. That's the day Fiona Dulaney was killed, isn't it?"

Once again, his telephone rang on cue and, ever the conscientious employee, Brian was compelled to answer it.

Eliza gave him a little wave. He stared helplessly after her as she cut through the restaurant to the kitchen. The food and beverage department was located in a large room with a long glass wall separating it from the kitchen. Since F & B oversaw the restaurant and all of the inn's private functions, the glass wall came in handy. The 'set-up' crew—including Tommy's friend Barry—arranged furniture and audio-visual equipment in the inn's private-function rooms. They might set up an intimate rehearsal dinner for the dozen members of a bridal party or a theater-style conference for two hundred business people.

Eliza spotted Wanda Johnson, the F & B secretary, through the glass wall. The managers must have been busy elsewhere.

This was good news. Eliza wouldn't have dared to ask many questions around the managers. On the other hand, Wanda had been at the inn about five years, ever since she graduated from high school. She knew all the employees and was a fount of information.

Wanda looked up with a gamin grin from the pile of papers she was working on. "Eliza, how's it going?"

"Fine," she replied. "Sorry to interrupt, but I was wondering whether you could help me out with something."

"Hey, they have me doing three things at once most of the time, anyway," Wanda said matter-of-factly, pushing her short wispy, blond hair behind her ears.

Wanda's plump, snub-nosed face with its perpetual dimpled grin reminded Eliza of a cherub. In fact, Wanda's looks were appropriate since she was a kind of female cupid, a matchmaker with her finger on the pulse of every romance at the inn. Months ago, Eliza had decided that Wanda fell into that category of hotel or inn employee who was so involved in the hotel life she had no outside life to speak of.

Eliza watched Wanda separate two attached pieces of paper, putting one in a pile to her left and one in a pile to her right. "Is Barry around?"

"Barry?" Wanda kept working on her piles of paper, but she gave Eliza a speculative glance. "He's gone for the day. He and the rest of the crew finished setting up the ballroom half an hour ago. You're not interested in Barry are you?"

Eliza shook her head adamantly. "No. I've been thinking about the murder. There's a good chance that someone here at the hotel knows something and doesn't even realize it. I was hoping that Barry's friend, Tommy, would be with him. Tommy might know something because he was working in the restaurant last Friday."

Eliza sat down on one of the chairs in front of Wanda's desk and leaned toward Wanda, lowering her voice to just above a whisper. "Do you know that on Friday—the day Fiona was killed—she had lunch with a guy who looks like Brad Pitt and no one seems to know this man's identity?"

Wanda's hands were still. "H-m-m, I wonder who he was? Fiona was dating a young doctor, a resident at the University of Virginia Hospital, but he was kind of a geek—nothing like Brad Pitt." Then, her eyes opened wide. "You think this Brad Pitt guy could be the killer?"

Eliza had to stifle a smile at Wanda's bug-eyed expression. "Maybe. The point is: we need to find this guy and go from there."

Wanda's forehead creased so that she looked like a worried child. "Isn't that a job for the police?"

Eliza sat back in her chair and crossed her arms impatiently. "Everyone knows that the police couldn't conduct their investigations without help from private citizens. As soon as we have factual information, we'll pass it along. You have the advantage of being an insider, in my view an especially knowledgeable one. Think about it!"

In a male-dominated department, Wanda was used to being the lowest 'man' on the totem pole. Clearly flattered by Eliza's confidence in her powers, Wanda didn't need any more convincing. She rested her forearms over her papers and leaned across her desk toward Eliza. "What can I do?"

Eliza studied Wanda's eager face with satisfaction. "Find out who this guy is. Ask Tommy about him. But—perhaps more importantly—find out whether anybody saw Fiona Dulaney after two o'clock last Friday."

Eliza felt a surge of excitement. Wanda was on her side! If Wanda couldn't find some answers, nobody could.

Chapter 8

The next afternoon, Eliza ambled along the northern perimeter of the inn's main building, staring down pensively at the flagstone sidewalk. She was just returning from the inn's lodging wing, having timed the walk between the front desk and Room 123. It had taken a rushed four minutes.

On Friday, the 'Do Not Disturb' sign had been placed on the doorknob when she made her return trip, say 12 to 15 minutes after the first fateful trip. That meant the murder probably had taken place between 4:35 and 4:50 p.m.

She had recorded the one-way estimation and her surmises about the approximate time of death in her notebook, but she didn't feel as if she'd learned anything new. It was cold but, finally, the sun had made an appearance. She gave herself a mental shake. One more stab at detecting and then she'd go down to the lake to feed the geese and swans.

Now, what would Kinsey Millhone—Eliza's favorite Sherlock and the star of Sue Grafton's best-selling mystery novels—do next? Eliza thought about the first title in the series, "A is for Alibi." *Ah ha! Establish alibis.* Jordan, Devin and Johnny were all verifiably elsewhere around the time of the murder. Of course, she would need to confirm their alibis. This brought Eliza up short. How was she to obtain and confirm alibis for the more than one hundred employees of the inn? She needed to concentrate on the most-likely 'perps'—short for perpetrators—as her favorite detective would say.

Eliza saw that she'd come full circle. She was no closer to

answering the same question dangling before her. Who would want to kill Fiona? Devin thought a jewel thief was the perpetrator, but Eliza had heard nothing about a forced entry. Besides, the thief would need to be familiar with Devin's unusual habit of keeping her gems in her possession. Again, Eliza wondered who would want Fiona dead and realized she didn't know enough about Fiona to even guess. Devin, on the other hand, was Fiona's college roommate and best friend for four years. Eliza lifted her gaze from the flagstones and her steps quickened as she strode purposefully toward the front desk.

She was in luck. The afternoon check-in rush was over, and Devin was seated in front of a quiet telephone switchboard. On the far side of the front desk area, Johnny was inputting some data into the computer. For once, Eliza was grateful for his habitual unfriendliness and for the fact that he didn't even deign to acknowledge her presence.

Devin swiveled toward her with a warm greeting and pulled out a chair, patting the seat.

Eliza accepted the invitation with alacrity. "It's still cold, but the sun's finally come out. In a few minutes I'm going to get some stale bread from the kitchen and go feed the geese and swans."

A smile brightened Devin's perfect features. "You lucky thing. Here I am stuck in the pit, as usual."

The front desk staff half-jokingly referred to their working area as 'the pit,' meaning that's where the real sweat and toil of the lodging business took place. While other inn staff had limited exposure or responsibility to guests, the front desk performed the 'dirty-work' of handling all the face-to-face needs, requests and complaints of guests—no matter how bizarre. Eliza looked around at the brown carpet, dark furnishings and wood-paneled walls, which half swallowed the weak fluorescent lighting. The area was like a pit—or a cave—in more ways than one, but she wasn't here to discuss the gloominess of the front desk.

"Devin, you probably think I'm nuts—and, if this is too painful, let me know—but I can't get Fiona off my mind. What was she really like?" Eliza asked.

Devin said nothing and her face was unreadable. Eliza was feeling like an insensitive jerk when Devin reached under the switchboard console and pulled out her purse. She removed her wallet and flipped it open, exposing a two by three-inch photograph. Eliza peered closely. Devin and Fiona stood with their arms around each other's shoulders and their heads together—long, strawberry-blond curls mingling.

On the several occasions when Eliza had seen Fiona at the hotel, she had received a definite impression of beauty. Now, gazing at Fiona and Devin side by side, she could see that her impression had been wrong. While Devin's features were beautifully symmetrical, Fiona's slanted, cat-like green eyes were set off by a long, narrow nose and a thin-lipped mouth. Still, there was no missing the charm beneath Fiona's radiant smile.

"Tell me about her," Eliza said. This time she wanted to know for herself. She would have made the same request even if she were not trying to determine a killer's motivations.

Devin smiled gently, a faraway look on her face as she studied the photograph. "Underneath that laughing, carefree exterior was a child-like vulnerability. Her father loved her and gave her whatever she wanted, but he wasn't there most of the time. She had no siblings and she lost her mother when she was small, you know."

Eliza hadn't known, but she nodded her head encouragingly.

"I remember going to parties with her. Guys would come up to us and ask if we were sisters," Devin said.

Eliza nodded again. "That makes sense. You hung around together constantly and you both had the same gorgeous hair."

Devin's face lost its faraway expression. "Yes, we were together a lot. But Fiona's hair color and curls were the product of a top-notch salon."

Eliza's eyes widened. "You mean she copied your hair?"

"Look, Fiona didn't do it to annoy me or anything. She was just used to pleasing herself."

Eliza frowned. Fiona must have coveted her friend's hair, and she didn't let Devin's feelings stand in her way. "She sounds disgustingly selfish."

"Oh, she was self-centered, but completely charming at the same time. Everyone wanted to be Fiona's friend. She was funny and smart, always laughing. And she was generous, inviting friends for weekends at her luxurious home or the family ski lodge or beach cottage. She'd spent her childhood at elite boarding schools and camps. She knew how to ride horseback, play tennis, ski and swim like a professional, but, at home, there was no one to ride with or play with or whatever," Devin said.

"Who were the close friends Fiona invited for weekends at her home? Was there anyone she might have offended?" Eliza asked.

"There was a core group of friends, three other girls besides myself. I could make a list, but, honestly, Fiona kept things light. No one ever was upset with her for long. I visited more than anyone, and often I was the only guest," Devin said.

Across the room, Johnny Burnett slammed a drawer shut with unnecessary force. It was as if a rifle had been fired in the small confines of the front desk. Eliza and Devin glanced over at him in surprise. He rose from his chair and stalked stiffly past them and out the swing door leading to the kitchen.

Devin shrugged her shoulders and rolled her eyes a little as if to say—Moody guy! What can you do?

Eliza wasn't going to let Johnny put her off stride. She was eager to hear the answer to her next question. "What about current friendships? What were her new friends like?"

"Fiona graduated only about a year ago. She was so busy with her business, she didn't really make any new friends worth mentioning."

Eliza was disappointed. No new leads. Then she realized that the silence was growing, so she asked the first inane question that popped into her head.

"Back in your college days when you visited Fiona's home, did you get to do a lot of horseback riding?"

Devin shook her head. "Unlike Miss Fiona Dulaney and many of the other Sweet Briar girls, I didn't have multiple trusts made out in my name the moment I was born. My riding background consisted of mucking about with a neighbor's 20-year-old, arthritic mare. Fiona, on the other hand, rode since she was big enough to sit in the saddle and took lessons from the best trainers in the country. Our Sweet Briar friends weren't in Fiona's league, but they'd had their share of lessons. I tried riding with them once, but I couldn't begin to keep up."

There was that sour tone again. This time, Eliza could understand its origins. From a distance, it was relatively easy to accept that someone had more advantages than you. Once you were close friends and you could examine every privilege and what the person had done differently than you to deserve it, you might be resentful.

The switchboard hummed. Devin pressed the lighted button and was soon involved in answering sightseeing questions. Eliza tuned Devin out with ease, her mind employed elsewhere. It was not Fiona Dulaney's advantages that captured her attention. Fiona's wealth was old news. In fact, until now, she had viewed Fiona as a stereotypical rich and spoiled young woman. Now she saw someone more complex.

Eliza could imagine Fiona's loneliness only too well. Like Fiona, she had only one hardworking parent and no siblings. She, too, knew about the hollow feeling that comes from growing up without one of your parents, having lost that parent when you were too small to even remember him or her properly. She couldn't imagine, however, being sent away to boarding school. Despite her mother's dedication to her job, she and her mother were a team. And because they moved so often, the mother-daughter bond was strengthened while Eliza's friendships tended to grow only the shallowest of roots.

Unlike Fiona's friendships. Eliza pictured a small Fiona at boarding school, far away from her father and achingly lonely. It would make sense if Fiona formed strong friendships at school. The same behavior would continue once Fiona was in college, explaining the bond between her and Devin.

Eliza thought about the bond that was developing between Sydney and herself. Sydney was the first friend who had managed to break through Eliza's self-protective shell. Every time Eliza faced a new town and a new set of peers, she made a promise to be true to herself. If people didn't like her, it wasn't the end of the world. She didn't exist to have friends. She could make her own happiness. The trouble was her independent attitude seemed to make her less approachable.

Then, this year, Sydney had taken Eliza under her wing. Sydney was always looking for Eliza at school and calling or visiting her at home. Syd had a charming, outgoing personality and the attention was flattering. Perhaps too flattering. Eliza cringed mentally when she thought about the cigarette incident. It would be so nice to belong for once, but at what cost? Sydney was doing her best to help, kind of like a big sister.

Eliza grew perfectly still. She knew why Fiona had dyed and permed her hair to resemble Devin's. Fiona wasn't trying to compete with her beautiful friend, or at least that wasn't her only motive. She wanted to express outwardly what she felt inwardly. To Fiona, Devin was a sister.

Eliza entered the kitchen with the intention of finding some bread for the geese and swans. She heard voices coming from the opposite side of the tall bread racks she was facing. One voice she recognized as belonging to T.J., a young bellman. The other voice was a deep rumble she couldn't identify.

"Wanda's been asking us about Fiona Dulaney. Some man took her to lunch here the day she was killed. Do you know anything about that?" asked T.J.

"Wanda's probably asked everybody 'bout it. Man, I wouldn't want to be in this guy's shoes. Unn Uhh. No way, no how," the deep voice said.

Then the voices began moving, coming closer. Eliza glanced frantically around for a less exposed listening post. Spotting the open walk-in meat freezer, she dashed over and slipped inside, moving just out of sight. It was cold, but she could hear their conversation without any risk of being spotted.

There was a 'ker-chink' as T.J. punched his card in the time clock. "Are you saying the man's guilty?"

"Guilty as sin, brother. Guilty as sin," deep voice stated.

"Come on, Franky. That's—what d'ya call it? Circumstantial. Where's your evidence, bro?"

"Hey, I seen these two in a serious argument just a couple days before she was killed," the deep-voiced Franky said.

"How do you know it was him? I mean, it coulda been some other dude," T.J. responded.

"Look, I know she was good lookin' and rich, but how many Brad Pitt doubles you think she hangs with?"

"So the guy you saw arguing with her looked like Brad Pitt? Man-oh-man, that's wild. Have you told Wanda?" T.J.'s voice was squeaky with excitement.

"No way. This is just between you and me. I don't volunteer any more than I have to. Know what I mean? 'Sides, like you said, bro, where's the evidence? But I know man, I know," Franky said.

There was a sudden rush of air and Eliza was standing in the dark. For a moment, she stood stock still in dull surprise. Then she leapt for the freezer door. It was closed, immovable. She ran her hands along its cold, perfectly smooth surface. No knob, no handle and no way out.

Chapter 9

Eliza banged against the door until her hands hurt. It was dark, and the pungent odor of raw meat filled her nostrils. Worst of all was the penetrating cold. She crossed her legs and wrapped her arms over her chest, tucking her hands under her upper arms. After standing like a pretzel for several minutes, she wondered whether she should be moving. Should she jog in place to keep warm? Would that use up too much oxygen? Was there a limited supply of oxygen within a freezer?

Eliza shivered, teeth chattering. Moron! She'd freeze to death before she used up the oxygen. A macabre image floated through her mind of her own white face frozen in a grimace, eyes bulging and clothes layered with ice. No! She wouldn't think like that. Of course, one of the kitchen staff would open the freezer soon.

As if her thoughts had magical powers, the door opened and light poured into the freezer. Eliza squinted at the cherub framed in the doorway. Then she came to her senses and rushed from the freezer into the splendid warmth of the kitchen.

"Th-thank you!" Eliza gasped through chattering teeth. "S-some helpful soul must have seen the open f-freezer and shut it, thinking they were s-saving energy."

"Good thing I was keeping an eye on things in the kitchen, as usual," Wanda said. "Otherwise you might be a popsicle by the time you got out."

Eliza's frozen cheeks began to burn. "You mean you saw me..."

Wanda's eyes twinkled and her dimples flashed. "I saw you

scamper into the refrigerator so you could eavesdrop on T.J. and Franky—shameless as a nosy, old woman! Then the phone rang and the next time I glanced over you were gone."

"Well, I did learn something very interesting," Eliza said.

Wanda's eyes bulged and she grabbed Eliza's arm and guided her to the food and beverage office. It was empty, so they sat down in the first chairs they came to, the two in front of Wanda's desk.

By the time Eliza had finished recounting T.J. and Franky's conversation, Wanda's chubby cheeks wore red patches. "Wait till I get my hands on that Franky! 'No ma'am, I didn't see Fiona Dulaney at all the day she was killed,' he tells me just as nice as can be when I ask him about Fiona's lunch partner. Never mind that he's spotted her arguing—arguing!—with Brad Pitt's double a couple days before her death!"

"Wanda, have you had any luck tracking down this Brad Pitt guy?" Eliza asked.

Wanda shook her head dejectedly. "Tommy is such a dim-bulb he couldn't even remember Fiona having lunch on Friday, much less give me any info about her companion. And, Eliza, more bad news. Fiona seems to have been invisible from the time she left the restaurant. To everyone except her killer, that is."

"Cheer up. Maybe Franky overheard something useful during that argument. Could you find out?"

Wanda's dimpled smile was wide, her naturally sunny outlook restored.

The following day, Eliza decided that, unlike Wanda, she would take a break from sleuthing. It was Friday, the school day was over and she was ready for an escape. Having obtained permission from her mother, Eliza slid behind the wheel of the station wagon, started it up and tuned the stereo to the University of Virginia, student-run rock-and-roll radio station. She smiled as a smooth male voice filled the car's interior, singing against the insistent throb of drums and an electric guitar. Her mother would catch a ride home with one of the sales staff. Eliza felt free as the wind.

She was on her way to meet Sydney and the gang at the movie theater. She wasn't wild about the movie choice, but even a horror film sounded good at this point. She pulled into a spot next to Sydney's red Honda, locked her mother's car carefully and strode over to the ticket booth. As soon as she walked into the lobby, she turned toward the sound of laughter and there were Sydney and Diana standing near the front windows having a wonderful time. Some of Eliza's ebullience drained away, but she scolded herself about being more positive. Perhaps she was just imagining Diana's antipathy toward her.

"Hi, Syd—Diana," said Eliza. "Whatever you're laughing about must be good."

Diana smirked. "You wouldn't get it, Liza Jane."

"Please call me Eliza," she said stiffly.

Diana continued to smirk. "Loosen up, E-liza. You are kind of little."

Eliza felt feverish. Diana must be referring to the folk song, "Little Liza Jane." Eliza didn't like being small and she liked being called 'little' even less.

Sydney grasped Eliza by the lower arm. "Eliza and I'll go save a bunch of seats. Diana, do you mind lookin' out for everybody?"

Sydney didn't bother waiting for Diana's agreement. She headed out of the lobby toward the theater rooms in the back of the building, tugging Eliza after her.

"Whew! You should have seen your face," Sydney said,

stopping next to the only unoccupied row of seats in the middle of the theater. After draping their jackets across three seats, Sydney took the aisle seat and Eliza sat just inside.

"How would you have felt, Syd?" Eliza asked, once they were sitting down. "She was insulting me, baiting me. I was looking at that purple lipstick of hers and seeing red when you dragged me off. I wouldn't have gone with you, except popping her in the mouth didn't seem like a smart move."

"She would have just loved makin' you sink to her level," Sydney said. "Uh oh, here they come."

Eliza and Sydney retrieved their jackets and moved to the inside. Eliza was grateful to be several seats removed from Diana.

The lights dimmed and the giant screen in front of them burst into life. Normally, Eliza avoided horror films. Even the vampire shows on television gave her nightmares. When the movie was almost over and it looked like the heroine was about to be transformed into a werewolf, Eliza decided to leave, whispering to Sydney that she was headed to the ladies'. All the girls turned sideways so that she could squeeze past except for Diana who didn't move a muscle. Eliza brushed swiftly past in case Diana decided to trip her.

The lobby was deserted except for the plump girl behind the snack counter reading a magazine. As she gazed out the front windows, Eliza saw Devin walking toward the theater. She did a double take and her pulse started to race. Walking beside Devin, holding her hand, was a man who bore a distinct resemblance to Brad Pitt.

When the couple entered the lobby, Devin spotted Eliza and strolled over to the windows, bringing her date along.

"Hi, Eliza. This is Derek Russell," said Devin. She turned

to the tall man with the familiar, appealing face. "Derek, this is Eliza Derby. I've mentioned her several times. She visits me at the front desk and helps relieve the stress or the boredom, whichever the case may be. Her mother is the Silver Fox's sales director."

"Nice to meet you, Eliza," said Derek, flashing a dazzling smile.

"What movie did you see?" Devin asked, while Eliza was staring at Derek's white teeth and masculine dimples.

Eliza switched her gaze to Devin. "I came with some friends and they wanted to see 'The Werewolf at Sand Glass Lake.' I'm afraid I left early, but the movie should be ending pretty soon."

"Not your favorite type of movie?" Derek asked sympathetically.

Eliza shook her head, absently. "Not to change the subject, but you look familiar."

Devin tucked her hand under Derek's arm. "Everyone who's seen a Brad Pitt film thinks he looks familiar."

"It's not that. I could have sworn I saw you at the Silver Fox Inn last Friday," Eliza said, the lie coming out as silky-smooth as Colin's orange flan.

"You probably did," Derek said. "Fiona Dulaney invited me to have lunch with her there. Her father's purchased some land recently for residential development. I'm a builder, and Fiona was trying to get me involved."

"I introduced Derek to Fiona," Devin said, her normally well-modulated voice oddly sharp.

Eliza kept her gaze on Derek's face. "After lunch, did you and Fiona go out to look at her father's land or anything?" she asked.

"No, things hadn't progressed that far. I left right after lunch,"

Derek said.

"Did Fiona mention what her plans were for the afternoon? Was she meeting anyone?" Eliza asked.

"I don't think so," Derek responded, forehead wrinkling. "Fiona certainly wasn't in a hurry. She wanted to order dessert, and I couldn't. I had paperwork to attend to—a bid I was putting together."

Eliza had been watching him closely. Unlike his celebrity look-alike, he was rather formal and stiff, but he seemed perfectly natural, completely at ease. Her next question could change that.

"Did you know that she was killed later that day?"

Derek stiffened, staring at her. "On the same day we had lunch together... She was joking and laughing—telling me these crazy stories about her jewelry business. It's horrible to think...."

Eliza wished she was better at reading faces. Derek seemed genuinely shocked, but maybe he was just an excellent actor.

Devin, who had been unusually silent, gave Derek's arm a tug. "We'd better go snag some seats. You know how crowded Friday nights are," she said with a strained smile.

Eliza was puzzled as the stunning pair hurried off, Devin tugging Derek along behind her. Devin was acting strangely. She hadn't even said good-bye.

Chapter 10

On Saturday morning, Eliza lay in bed, savoring the fact that today she didn't have to hurry off to school or to the inn. Thoughts of the evening before drifted through her mind. Why had Devin been so uncharacteristically tense and nervous? Then, it dawned on Eliza. Perhaps Devin hadn't known about Derek having lunch with Fiona. She would have been hurt to find out from a third party.

Today, Eliza was supposed to go shopping with Sydney and the gang. Diana would be there. How was she going to deal with her? She would just have to play it by ear, but she couldn't let Diana push her around.

Eliza rolled out of bed, determined to ignore any flickers of reluctance or trepidation. She showered, dressed and did her hair and makeup, all the while concentrating on how much fun shopping with her friends would be. Afterwards, they could all have lunch or an ice-cream cone.

She surveyed herself in the mirror. Jeans, turtleneck, blazer and boots that added a much needed two inches. Long hair vigorously brushed and left hanging over one shoulder. Her lashes were so dark she never bothered with mascara, but she'd added a touch of blush and lipstick. If only she looked older. She twisted a bright scarf into a choker around her neck. That was better. She fingered the scarf as a faintly uneasy feeling swept over her.

The doorbell chimed. She grabbed her handbag, ran down the stairs and hurried to open the door. Sydney stood there, smiling sweetly, blond hair shining in the sunlight.

Kristen was sitting in the front passenger seat of Sydney's two-door Honda. She jumped out and pulled the seat forward so that Eliza could climb into the back. Fifteen minutes later they pulled into the parking lot at the Barracks Road Shopping Center. Diana and Amanda were waiting for them at a large round, stonewalled fountain.

Their first stop was the A & N Store. While Sydney tried on several pairs of athletic shoes, the others wandered about looking at Levi's, sweats and the new spring clothes including casual skirts, jumpers and tops. When Sydney strolled to the checkout line, everyone began gathering at the front of the store.

Eliza was admiring a front-counter display of inexpensive jewelry when Kristen appeared at her elbow. Without a word, the curly-haired brunette reached over and picked up a pair of silver earrings. She studied them for several moments before dropping them into her capacious pocketbook. At first, Eliza thought it was an accident. Then she observed Kristen surreptitiously zipping the purse.

Her stomach tightened. What was she supposed to do? She wanted to tell Kristen to put the earrings back pronto, but there were a couple of sales clerks close-by. Normal conversation would be overheard and whispering could draw attention.

After making her purchase, Sydney headed toward the doors and the other girls followed, Eliza trailing behind. Sydney held a door open for them, then fell into step beside Eliza.

"Hey, Eliza," she said. She stopped to pull the shoebox from her bag and open the lid. "Look what I found. Marked down twice. They were a steal!"

Eliza winced at the word 'steal.' She peered into the box at the white sneakers, trimmed in purple and Day-Glo orange. No wonder they were on sale.

"What's the matter? You don't like them?" Sydney asked, a hurt expression on her face.

"Sorry, Syd. I was thinking about something else," Eliza responded. She started to confide in Sydney when Diana sauntered up.

The tall girl glanced over Sydney's shoulder. "Wow! Do they glow in the dark? I've got just the outfit to go with them. Let me break them in for you, Syd."

Sydney shook her head. "No way. You'd break them in all right. The last time you borrowed my shoes, Di, I didn't get them back till they had holes."

"You're exaggerating," Diana scoffed, lightly.

"I'm not exaggeratin' even one teeny bit," Sydney stated.

They were following Kristen and Amanda into the CVS/Pharmacy store. The girls scattered in different directions, disappearing down the maze-like aisles. Eliza stayed to herself. The same question kept echoing within her head. What should she do about Kristen? She needed some hair conditioner, but she stared sightlessly at a plethora of shampoos, deep conditioners, daily conditioners, gels and sprays. After ten minutes, she went outside and sat on a concrete bench.

What should she do about Kristen's shoplifting? Perhaps she shouldn't confide in Sydney. It smacked of being a rat. Maybe she should just confront Kristen.

Amanda and Kristen came out—Amanda giggling and Kristen cackling away like a witch. Eliza scooted over on the bench to make room. A couple minutes later Sydney and Diana joined them.

"Y'all interested in goin' to Peace Frogs?" Sydney asked.

Everybody was enthusiastic, so they trooped past Hot Cakes, Eliza's favorite bakery. Peace Frogs was small compared to CVS and there were no long aisles down which Eliza could disappear. T-shirts in a startling rainbow of colors hung from the ceiling to the floor. Eliza bought a tie-dyed shirt in gorgeous shades of blue with the ubiquitous frog emblem holding up two fingers in friendly greeting. Now, she'd spent her limit with just enough money left over for lunch, but she was in a much more positive mood.

Surely Kristen's theft was a one-time deal, she told herself. Probably Kristen had never shoplifted before and never would again. Most likely, she was riddled with guilt. Eliza conveniently ignored the way Kristen and Amanda had been giggling conspiratorially throughout the morning.

The group huddled on the sidewalk outside of Peace Frogs. Diana and Sydney were ready for lunch. Besides the bakery, Hot Cakes had a wonderful deli and there was a spacious area with tables and chairs. On the other hand, Casella's Italian Restaurant had delicious pizza by the slice. When Kristen suggested stopping at the nature store next to Casella's before lunch, pizza won out.

Eliza slowed her steps to match Sydney's relaxed stroll. The wind had picked up and she balled her hands into her blazer pockets wishing that she'd brought her jacket and that Sydney walked faster. Finally, they reached the store and bells clattered as they entered.

The young woman behind the counter smiled and said good morning. The girls murmured their greetings in return.

Eliza began by listening to a couple of compact discs, one with the sounds of falling water and birdcalls and the other celebrating Native American music. When Kristen and Amanda came over, she headed to the back of the store. When she'd tired of looking at nature-oriented books, toys and cards, she strolled over to the jewelry section in the middle of the store.

There were lovely necklaces, bracelets and earrings made

from shells and semi-precious stones. She spent a long time admiring the hair ornaments, especially a silver barrette in the shape of a galloping horse. The barrette was large enough to contain her thick hair and it would look great with her silver-buckled black belt.

Sydney appeared at her elbow and noticed the focus of her interest. "Go for it. That looks just like you."

Eliza shook her head. "I've spent my money. What about you? Find anything you like?"

Sydney nodded and smiled. "You know me. I'm just tryin' to make up my mind what I like best."

Sydney wandered off and Eliza moved over to a long, narrow table filled with necklaces. Kristen and Amanda joined her, one on each side.

"That music's s'posed to be real peaceful, but I wouldn't want to play it if I were alone in the house at night. I'd feel like some wild animal was going to get me," Amanda said.

Kristen grinned. "You're crazy, girl."

Amanda fingered a lovely silver and turquoise necklace. She pulled it toward her, burying it in her fist. Eliza tensed. A moment later, Amanda's fist slid from the table to her pants pocket. Eliza stared at Amanda's face, then flicked her gaze toward Kristen.

She felt sick when the brunette smirked and winked. It was happening again, only this was worse. The two girls were including her in their conspiracy, as if she would find it clever and amusing.

"That's funny," a woman said from directly behind them.

Eliza jerked and looked around. There was the nice sales clerk, staring at the three girls. Eliza felt branded.

"I could have sworn there was a silver and turquoise necklace right about here," and she pointed to the rectangle of space where the necklace used to lie. "Whenever there's a sale, I try to rearrange the display," the young woman explained. Her mouth turned up in a smile, but her eyes were no longer friendly. With slow deliberation, she strode toward the sales counter and the telephone.

Kristen put a hand over her mouth to smother a nervous cackle. Amanda's face, always pale, looked like chalk. Keeping her gaze on the back of the sales clerk's head, Amanda stuffed her plump hand into her jeans pocket, yanked the necklace out and dropped it onto its original spot. Then she made a swift exit with Kristen not far behind. Eliza stared at the delicate silver and turquoise strand tangled into a clumsy heap before she, too, decided to leave. Would she ever feel comfortable in this store again?

That evening she was sitting at the desk in her room working on a science project when the doorbell rang.

"E-li-za," her mother cried.

Eliza ran to the top of the stairs and there was Sydney standing just inside the door. Her mother was already disappearing into the kitchen. Eliza came down the steps slowly with none of her usual enthusiasm at seeing her friend.

Sydney's sunny smile faded. "Hey, Eliza. Can we talk?"

The two girls walked in silence to Eliza's room. Out of habit, they plopped down onto the rug. Sydney reached into her handbag, withdrew a silvery object and handed it to Eliza. It was the barrette from Nature by Design. Eliza was amazed by how the artisan had transmitted the fluid grace of a galloping horse onto the small piece of silver. How thoughtful and generous of Sydney. In a burst of warm feelings, Eliza hugged her friend and some of her disgust with the morning's shopping excursion melted away.

Sydney returned the hug and then sat back. "Whew! I sure am glad to see that sad look disappear from your face."

Eliza's joy dimmed somewhat. "How well do you know Kristen and Amanda?"

"Well, I see them practically every day," Sydney responded. "What do you mean?"

Eliza hesitated. "They took or tried to take little things from a couple of the stores today. Syd, they were shoplifting."

Sydney's face was unreadable. "So, what did they take?"

"Kristen took earrings at A & N and Amanda slipped a necklace into her pocket at the nature store but, after the sales girl came over, she put it back."

"Gee, I thought you were going to tell me they'd stolen a couple of diamonds or somethin'. The store'll never even miss what Kristen took and Amanda didn't end up takin' a thing. What's the big deal?" Sydney asked.

Eliza felt as if the room was tilting and she was off balance. "For all I know they might've taken other things, but that's not the point. Sydney—they were stealing."

"Come on, Eliza. You're bein' awful judgmental," Sydney said, irritation sharpening her normal soft drawl.

"You act like being judgmental is worse than being a thief!" Eliza exclaimed, jumping to her feet.

"There you go again. All holier than thou," Sydney scoffed, rising from the carpet more slowly.

Eliza wanted to smack her friend's patronizing face. Instead, she buried her hands in her pockets.

"Look, I came over to cheer you up and here we are havin' an argument. How about showin' me how you tied that pretty scarf you're wearin' instead? When I tie a scarf, it looks okay for about ten seconds," Sydney said.

"E-li-za, tele-pho-one," her mother shouted up the stairs.

"Thank you!" Eliza called, then she turned to Sydney. "I'll be right back."

She hurried to the phone in her mother's room. "Hello," she said breathlessly.

"Hi, this is Joe," a friendly, confident voice said. "Would you like to go ice skating next weekend?"

Eliza smiled. "Sure."

"How about Saturday afternoon?" Joe asked. "I could pick you up around two o'clock."

"Saturday afternoon sounds great. I'll just double-check with my mom." Before Eliza could set down the phone, Joe began speaking enthusiastically.

"By the way, I really enjoyed reading your stuff, especially that story about the trail ride. There's no doubt about it—you can write."

"Thanks," she said softly, a warm glow suffusing her body. Then, out of the corner of her eye, she spotted movement across the hall. "Syd's here, so I should run, but Saturday shouldn't be a problem. I'll let you know when I see you at school on Monday."

"Sounds good," Joe said. "Have a great weekend, Eliza."

"You, too," Eliza said.

After she hung up the phone, she was still breathless, and she sat there for a moment anticipating her first real date with Joe. When she entered the bedroom, her friend was standing in front of her open closet perusing its contents. Eliza knew the louvered doors were shut when she left the room.

"Hey, Eliza," Sydney said. "Why don't you ever wear any of these gorgeous dresses?"

Sydney had stepped inside Eliza's personal boundaries, but Eliza contained her annoyance because there had been enough tension already. "They're a little dressy for school. Come on,

I'll show you my scarf-tying tricks."

Eliza selected two oblong scarves and handed one to Sydney. Then she demonstrated her folding and tying techniques step-by-step while Sydney imitated her. On the third attempt, Sydney's scarf formed a neat choker around her neck. The scarf's jewel-bright colors gave her navy sweater a sophisticated look.

"That's great! Wear it home, if you like," Eliza said, eager to please her friend and restore their relationship to its normal, easy footing.

Sydney smiled sunnily. "Thanks, Eliza. You're a wonderful teacher. You're a terrific friend, too. Just don't take everything so seriously!"

She gave Eliza a hug, grabbed her jacket and her oversized, bucket-style handbag and made her departure. From the shelter of the front porch, Eliza watched the red Honda drive off. She fingered the scarf at her neck, experiencing a prickle of uneasiness for the second time that day, as if she were forgetting something. As Sydney disappeared in the distance, Eliza's uneasiness was swept aside by a wave of anger and disappointment.

Now that Sydney was gone, Eliza's feelings gushed forth. Sydney had called her self-righteous and holier than thou. That had hurt and been so unexpected. In fact, Sydney's whole reaction to the news about Kristen and Amanda's shoplifting was unexpected. She thought it was no big deal. Maybe she knew already. Eliza sat down on the porch steps with a thump. Sydney had not been surprised. She did know about the shoplifting and, worse, she didn't care.

Eliza shivered. It was cold out on the porch. She returned to her bedroom. Lying on the bed was the lovely horse barrette. Despite all the other things that had gone wrong between Sydney and her today, here was something right. Sydney had been perceptive to realize how much Eliza coveted the barrette. Eliza plucked the hair ornament off the bed and went over to the belt rack in her still-open closet. It would go perfectly with her silver-buckled black belt. She reached out for the belt, but her hand landed on a tan belt instead. She put the barrette down and looked more closely. She owned only a handful of belts. Her favorite, the black belt with the unique silver buckle, was missing.

Chapter 11

The sun kept moving in and out of the clouds, the sky was a flickering smoky-blue and great gusts of cool air shook the bare tree branches and blew dead leaves and debris along the ground. Eliza inhaled deeply, but the soft scent of rain or snow was lost beneath the pungent smells of horse and earth and rotting leaves. There was an unsettled feeling as if a thunderstorm were brewing, yet a thunderstorm in early March seemed impossible. Eliza didn't mind because the wind contained none of the harsh chill of the preceding days and the rock-hard, frozen ground had softened enough for an enjoyable cross-country ride.

It was Sunday, and she and Red, the inn's big chestnut gelding, were on the return leg of a long trail ride, trotting along a well-worn path in the pasture behind the inn. The trail described a big circle beginning in the pasture, then meandering through the woods to a meadow with a large pond and finally returning back through the woods to the pasture. Eliza took quiet joy from observing her equine friend, sharing his enjoyment of the day, the surroundings and the release of pent-up energy.

She stopped posting and sat deep in the saddle, pressing her right leg into the gelding's side. He broke into a canter and, when she leaned forward and pressed both legs into his sides, he surged ahead into a flat-out gallop. Now the cool air whipped her cheeks and the trees and grass became a blur as they flew past. Eliza spotted their favorite jump, a hedge sitting in the middle of the fence line just ahead. She squared her shoulders and leaned back, reining the chestnut in and bringing his big body into balance.

She and her mount were eager yet relaxed as they headed straight toward the hedge. They flew up into the air but, instead of arcing smoothly over the hedge, Eliza felt Red's body jerk beneath her midway. Then she was airborne, sailing over his head and plummeting toward the ground.

Eliza couldn't breathe. She lay on her back, staring up at the swirling clouds in fear. She called Red's name but all that came out was a pitiful squeak. She took another deep breath and this time her lungs filled with sweet air and she coughed. The fall must have knocked the air right out of her. She sat up gingerly, looking for Red.

There he was, grazing nervously a few feet away. He would snatch a bite of grass then raise his head and gaze wild-eyed around him. Poor fellow, he didn't know what had happened. For that matter, neither did she. Eliza rose shakily to her feet and took a few feeble steps. Though her back ached, everything was in working order, so she continued over to Red, talking softly to him and holding out one of the sugar lumps she pilfered regularly from the inn. When the gelding reached for the sugar in her right hand, Eliza grabbed the reins with her left.

She drew the reins over his head, stroking his satiny neck and murmuring all the while. "Good boy. What a good boy. That sugar's so-o-o tasty."

Leading the gelding, she urged him into a fast walk followed by a trot. Although it was difficult to tell when she was moving beside him rather than observing from a distance, he didn't appear to be lame.

"Let's go take a look at the hedge and see if we can figure out why you fell," Eliza said, giving Red a couple more pats on the neck. Ostensibly, she was calming the gelding, but the sound of her own voice and the feel of Red's velvety, warm coat beneath her fingertips soothed her trembling nerve endings.

She led the gelding through a gate in the fence and around to the approach to the jump. Eliza gazed at the ground in front of the hedge. Nothing. Then she studied the hedge itself. Thinking her jangled nerves were effecting her vision, she saw something glittering along the top of the hedge just above the lacy evergreens. Shakily, Eliza walked toward the jump.

It wasn't until she was standing right in front of the hedge that she could find the source of the mysterious glitter. A thin, metal wire ran between the jump's two posts. Eliza touched the wire with an unsteady finger. Whenever she went trail riding, whether she was riding Red or another horse, she jumped this hedge. Someone must have known. Someone had been watching.

The wind kicked up again and the gelding moved restively. Eliza jerked his reins lightly. "Settle down, fella. I'll be through in a moment."

Eliza began unraveling the wire from the fence posts. Several tedious minutes passed and, with the help of her pocketknife, she succeeded finally in removing the wire. Then she wound it into a ball and stuffed it into a jacket pocket, nicking her finger in the process. Her eyes smarted and a hot burst of anger shot through her.

Eliza stared across the pasture at the back of the Silver Fox Inn. A man and a woman walking along the lake were the only people in sight. She gazed up at the buildings. So many windows.

She turned decisively toward her horse, mounted and eased him into a slow trot toward the stables. Having determined, once again, that Red was sound, she clucked to him and he picked up the pace.

Within an hour, Eliza was back at the inn. She wanted to confide in someone. Her mother would be frightened and would inform the police, effectively putting an end to Eliza's detecting. Telling Wanda would be like putting a notice on the employee bulletin board. Talking to Devin was a possibility, but, much as Eliza admired the beautiful older girl, she couldn't envision going to her for help.

Eliza hoped that Jordan would be available. He teased her like a big brother, but she trusted him. He was unfailingly honest, cool-headed and sensible with guests and other staff.

When Eliza entered the front desk area, Devin was seated at the switchboard in mid-conversation. Eliza slid past her and headed for the far side of the front desk where Jordan was typing at the computer.

"Jordan, I've got a problem," Eliza began, rolling one of the office chairs over next to him.

Jordan kept on typing, an amused smile tugging the corners of his mouth. "Hello, Eliza. How are you? Beautiful day, isn't it?"

"This is serious. I need to talk to you before we're interrupted," Eliza said.

Jordan swiveled toward her with a resigned sigh. "What is it?"

As Eliza described the accident at the hedge succinctly and undramatically, Jordan's resignation was replaced by concern.

"When I went over to the jump to investigate, this is what I found tied between the fence posts," Eliza said, glancing around to make sure no one was looking before pulling out the ball of wire.

"Wow," Jordan said in a hollow voice, holding the

scrunched-up wire in the palm of his hand. "This was malicious. Someone was aiming to do some damage."

"Yeah and that someone was after me," Eliza said. "Every time I go trail riding, I take that jump."

Jordan gave her a doubtful look. "You can't be sure of that, Eliza. Why would anyone go after you?"

"Because I've been asking a lot of questions about the murder," Eliza explained, her voice high-pitched and strained.

Jordan patted her tight shoulders. "Come on, Eliza. You're falling into the trap most people fall into. You're taking events personally. I don't mean to discredit you, but I doubt a murderer would take you too seriously."

Eliza could feel her face growing hot, and she struggled to keep her voice low. "Let me tell you about a little coincidence. A couple days ago, I was in the kitchen when I overheard this highly interesting conversation, and I needed a place to hide. So, I stepped into the big meat freezer."

Eliza noticed the way Jordan's eyebrow had begun to climb and his mouth was quivering. "Now, don't laugh! These two set-up guys were talking about Fiona Dulaney. Anyway, someone slammed the freezer door on me. If Wanda hadn't opened the door..."

Jordan held out his hands, palms raised. "Whoa, slow down, honey. If you could see your face—your nostrils are flaring with temper. I am doing my best here to keep an open mind. You say you were spying on a couple of F&B guys from inside the freezer and someone closed the door. That sounds accidental to me."

Eliza drew a deep, trembling breath, striving to keep her temper in check. It would be nice to be taken seriously for once. She gazed searchingly at her friend's handsome, coffee-colored face. "Are you a big believer in coincidences?"

Jordan was quiet for several moments, his mobile face still. "The freezer incident by itself doesn't give me pause. But, when I put it together with the wired fence, I feel a little less sanguine. Eliza, you need to report this."

Eliza blinked. She should have expected this reaction, but she hadn't. "I will report it, but I'd like to wait." She laid a hand on Jordan's arm as he started to speak. "If the police know or my mom, for that matter, I'll be forbidden to come to the hotel after school."

Jordan's mouth curled in a knowing, little grin. "Right, and you won't be able to stick your nose into a murder investigation which should, of course, be left to the police. Detective Thompson doesn't strike me as any kind of fool."

"You have no idea how lonely and boring it is at the cottage. I'll promise to stop asking questions, if you'll just keep this to yourself," Eliza pleaded.

"On one condition. If anything else happens, even the smallest thing, you're to tell me about it immediately and we'll go straight to your mother," Jordan said firmly, his cat-like, preternaturally intelligent eyes boring into hers.

Eliza nodded, solemnly. "Thanks, Jordan."

Jordan went back to work on the computer and she expelled a long sigh of relief. Then she glanced around. Devin was still busy at the switchboard. She was taking a reservation. Since the reservations department was closed on weekends, the front desk handled all lodging requests. Eliza realized she was thirsty and none too clean, so she got up from her seat and headed out.

As Eliza strode past the switchboard, Devin swiveled around. "Have you all heard the forecast?" she asked, raising her voice for Jordan's benefit.

Eliza shook her head as Jordan jumped up and strolled over to the switchboard. "A big ice storm is due to hit us some time tonight. Robert called to ask whether Jordan and I would be willing to stay over," Devin explained.

"Wow. I can't believe it," Eliza said. "I just came in from riding and it was so warm."

"Well, it's dropped ten degrees in the last hour and it's going to get a lot colder before it stops," Devin said.

The front desk phone rang and Jordan answered it. He spoke briefly before hanging up.

Jordan grinned at Eliza. "That was your mother. She wants to see you. My guess is you won't be seeing that boring old cottage of yours for a while, Eliza. Looks like we'll all be spending the night at the Silver Fox Inn."

Chapter 12

Eliza was freezing. She reached for her down comforter and touched a scratchy wool blanket instead. Opening her eyes, she gazed blearily at a colonial-style desk, a landscape mirror above a matching bureau and, across from her, another bed with a lump under the covers. Judging by the swath of silvery-blond hair emerging at the top, the lump was her mother. She and her mother had gone to bed late last night after dining at the inn's highly rated restaurant.

Pulling the blanket around her shoulders, Eliza sat up and swung her legs to the floor. The plush, wool carpet was cool beneath her feet as she pattered over to the window. Fairyland. The ground was powdered with snow, like a generous sprinkling of confectioners sugar decorating a cake. Everything sparkled as if bewitched in the sunlight. Bushes and trees, the roofline of the inn's main building, the garden gazebo, the small storage shed and the cars. Then Eliza spotted her favorite tree, a small Dogwood, bent over as if taking a bow. Finally, it hit her. A heavy coating of ice burdened the dogwood and added that magical sparkle to the tree and every other object within sight.

As Eliza gazed at the ice-encased landscape, she realized that something was missing. No machines sputtered and roared; no people spoke or laughed. Somehow, the scene made more of an impact surrounded by this hush. It was as if a spell had been cast upon the Silver Fox Inn, sending everyone except Eliza into a deep sleep.

Suddenly, Eliza was eager to get out and explore. Tossing

95

the blanket onto her bed, she hurried into the bathroom, rising on tiptoe as her feet hit the frigid tile floor and automatically flipping the light switch. Nothing happened. She flipped it up and down several times with the same result. She ran to the overhead light switch by the entrance door and flipped it up. Still nothing. Now the deep silence seemed less magical. The furnace wasn't blowing warm air and the electrical appliances weren't humming. The storm must have caused some damage to the power lines. She was shivering with cold.

"Eliza," her mother called, sleepily.

"Right here." Eliza darted back to the main room, jumped into bed and pulled the covers up around her.

Her mother sat up. "It's freezing. Did we forget to adjust the thermostat last night?"

Eliza shook her head. "Mom, the power's out. You should see all the ice outside. It's really beautiful."

Instead of running to the window, her mother lifted the telephone receiver and placed it next to her ear. "Hello, Martin? Do you have power? Well, at least the phones are working."

Eliza knew that Martin was the night auditor/late-shift front desk clerk. She watched her mother drop the telephone receiver back in its cradle and spring into action, swinging out of bed and talking as she dressed.

"The ice may be beautiful, but it's a major pain in the neck. Just imagine dealing with a hundred disgruntled guests."

Eliza's mother picked up her watch and began fastening it onto her wrist. "It's ten after seven. Check out the t.v. news... I mean, call the school emergency number."

By this time, Eliza was out of bed and pulling on the clothes she had worn yesterday. She knew the schools would be closed. The Charlottesville-area schools tended to shut down at the least hint of snow or ice. Since severe weather was an exception to the rule, Charlottesvillians—Southerners, after all—tended to panic. Plus, the local authorities were reluctant to invest in heavy snow and ice equipment that would be used only once every couple of years.

As she stood in front of the dressing area mirror, her purse comb snagging through the tangled length of her hair, she watched her mother applying make up. Her mother's hands were swift and sure. She was dressed in an elegant periwinkle suit, the spare outfit she always kept in her office for emergencies like this one. Her pageboy was a little less full than usual, but still looked neat and stylish. Eliza wrinkled her nose at her own well-creased jeans and the tiny smear of chocolate on the neck of her sweater.

Although Eliza fantasized sometimes about being the sales director or the general manager of a hotel, she had no desire to trade places with her mother this morning. She discerned a brittle tension beneath her mother's polished, professional appearance and she had no intention of uttering a word unless absolutely necessary.

By silent mutual consent, Eliza and her mother left the room and strode swiftly down the deserted hall to the stairs. There were no windows in the stairwell, but the emergency generator produced a dim, blue light.

When they reached the lobby, Eliza was delighted to see a large table set up with coffee, juice, muffins and danish. She grabbed a juice and cinnamon roll then trotted after her mother through the door marked 'Private' to the front desk.

Well away from the front desk window, Jordan and Robert Avery hovered over a stack of papers. When Jordan spotted Eliza and her mother, he nodded politely without a trace of his usual whimsical good spirits.

Robert smoothed a nervous finger over his small mustache.

"Contact these folks and find out whether they'd like us to secure a room for them at the Jefferson Inn. Right now, it's one of the few hotels with electricity so the vacancies won't last long."

"Should I book a room for them as soon as I get their approval?" Jordan asked.

Robert shook his head. "I've reserved a block of rooms, but there won't be enough for everybody. Compile a list of who wants to switch, and I'll take over from there. Move quickly, Jordan. We've got a lot of ground to cover."

Jordan picked up the telephone receiver and began punching room numbers. Eliza's mother and Robert disappeared into the office. Eliza stayed where she was, curious to see how the front desk staff would deal with the ice storm's aftermath.

Eliza watched with fascination as Jordan smiled into the mouthpiece of the telephone. A moment ago, he had looked more tense and gloomy than Eliza had ever seen him. Now, his voice was relaxed, friendly and amazingly upbeat as he explained the situation to a hotel guest.

Martin was manning the switchboard. Normally, he would be leaving about now. Like Jordan, he set aside his own concerns and put on his happiest voice for the guests. Three phone calls in quick succession involved the same question: When would the inn regain power? The answer varied slightly, but it amounted to the same thing: We don't know.

Devin stood in the front desk window, dealing with a queue of people filled with worries and complaints. A husky man in an 'I am my kid's dad' sweatshirt faced Devin from the other side of the desk.

"Our plane leaves at noon, so I requested some help with our luggage. The bellmen were busy assisting other guests," he explained, his round, heavily jowled face flushing with emotion.

"Since the elevators were out of order, I lugged suitcases plus the baby's travel bed, portable high chair and swing down two flights of stairs. Finally—my back spasming—I joined my family in the lobby, looking forward to a reward, your famous country breakfast—"

Devin, who had been listening respectfully to his tirade, neatly interrupted. "I understand how you feel, Mr. Simmonds. Eggs and bacon are much more satisfying than a continental breakfast. If we regain power, you should be able to have your hot breakfast immediately. Meanwhile, have you tried the muffins? Our baker is known for his scrumptious breads."

Devin smiled and her perfect features were shown to their best advantage. Eliza watched the disgruntled father return Devin's stunning smile before he strode away.

The person standing in line behind him was less likely to be influenced by Devin's feminine charm. A tall, skinny woman with large, prominent blue eyes and a bird's nest of frizzy, gray hair stepped up to the desk, pinning Devin with a suspicious gaze.

"Every one of my bones and joints is aching after being frozen all night. I'll never make it back up the stairs to my room. Could you please tell me when the power will return?" she asked in an accusing, but lady-like contralto.

"There are people working on the problem as we speak. Unfortunately, I cannot tell you exactly how long the repairs will take. The storm did a lot of damage to the entire area. Perhaps you might enjoy having coffee or tea in front of a nice, roaring fire. There's a fireplace in the Hunt Room, or, if you want someplace really quiet, try the library," Devin offered helpfully.

A hot, fireside drink seemed to appeal to the woman. She released Devin from her pop-eyed stare and moved off with her companions. Again and yet again a guest walked away from the front desk much calmer than when he or she arrived. Eliza marveled at Devin's mesmerizing, soothing charm.

She wondered how the rest of the hotel staff were coping. The hallway to the kitchen was strangely dark and quiet, as if it were three in the morning rather than nine. Likewise, entering the kitchen was a surreal experience. The kitchen—usually crashingly loud and full of activity all lit up by fluorescent lights—was relatively quiet and still with only the high bank of windows running the length of the outside wall admitting a soft, natural light. The chef and one of the food and beverage managers stood together chatting on the far side of the room. To Eliza's amazement, they were making expansive gestures, smiling and chuckling as if they hadn't a care in the world.

There was a skeleton crew filling juice pitchers and putting a tray of breakfast breads together. They went about their work cheerfully, talking and joking as if everything were quite normal. The rest of the staff must have been called off or stranded by the ice storm.

Eliza glanced toward the window of the food and beverage office, expecting to see a dark, empty room, but, to her surprise, Wanda was sitting at her desk in a pool of light. Eliza hurried over. Since Wanda didn't work on weekends, Eliza hadn't had a chance to tell her about Friday night.

"So, why didn't you get votive candles like everyone else?" Eliza asked, gazing at the large, camping-style lantern on Wanda's desk.

Wanda looked up—wide-eyed—the shadows only serving to emphasize the cherub-like roundness of her features. "Eliza— you scared me. It's kinda spooky around here. I brought the lantern from home, and, boy, am I glad I did!"

"Speaking of spooks and other bad guys, you'll never believe what happened when I went to the movies on Friday night," Eliza said, settling into one of the chairs in front of Wanda's desk. She described her encounter with Devin Cooper and Derek Russell.

"Devin was acting weird—kind of nervous and unfriendly," Eliza added.

Wanda rolled her eyes. "That's not weird for Devin. When she wants something, she's sweet as pie. Then later, when you come up to her expecting to be treated warmly, she'll snub you in a heartbeat if it suits her. She's as two-faced as they come."

Eliza was taken aback. "Except for Friday night, Devin has always gone out of her way to be nice to me."

"Well, she has her own selfish reasons. Count on it. After all, you are the sale's director's daughter." Then, as Eliza started to protest, she interrupted. "Forget about Devin. I'm curious about our Brad Pitt guy—Derek. He wasn't very helpful, was he?"

Eliza made a face. "No. He left right after lunch and he had no idea what her plans were for the rest of the afternoon."

"And it was so convenient that he had to rush off after lunch to work on a bid, probably by himself. You know what that means—no alibi."

Eliza nodded. "But, Wanda, he seemed perfectly relaxed and straight forward—not like he was hiding anything. He didn't even realize why I was asking all those questions."

"How do you know what he was thinking? He might have been lying, and we'd never know the difference," Wanda said.

"Yeah, I see what you mean," Eliza said. "I was just giving you my impression. I wouldn't dream of crossing him off the list of suspects."

"What list of suspects?" Wanda asked, sarcastically, but she was smiling.

"Hey, we're making progress here. We've got the identity of Fiona's mysterious lunch partner. And, you haven't told me what Franky had to say."

Wanda leaned across her desk toward Eliza, lowering her voice conspiratorially. "He was ready to give me the run around again, but I knew about a certain girl he took out on a date. Franky's married, you know. Anyway, according to Mr. Truthful, Derek and Fiona were very angry, especially Derek. Unfortunately, Franky was too far away to hear much, but a couple times Derek shouted at Fiona. Once he yelled 'Poor little rich girl' and the next time he shouted something like 'You're making a federal case out of this.'"

Eliza's pulse quickened. "Wow. That sounds like Fiona Dulaney knew something about Derek that could get him in trouble."

Wanda smiled smugly. "It does, indeed."

"Has Franky told the police about this?"

Wanda shook her head. "I'm sure he hasn't. This is strictly confidential, Eliza, but Franky's had a run in or two with the law before. He avoids cops as much as possible."

"Did he tell you anything else?" Eliza asked eagerly.

"Nothing. Still, what he did say was pretty thought provoking," Wanda said.

"I'll say! Great work, Wanda. Derek Russell could be our man."

Eliza's pulse was racing with excitement. This must be what it felt like to be a police detective or a private investigator.

Chapter 13

On Tuesday morning, Eliza was jolted from a sound sleep by her clattering alarm. Having switched off the offending instrument, she pattered over to the sunlit window. Only a few broken branches and damaged trees hinted at yesterday's storm. The grass was not tinted by even a touch of frost. She gazed upon a gentle spring day.

It was one of those rare mornings when her every movement was smooth and coordinated. She was ready for school in record time.

As she entered Albemarle High surrounded by a swarm of students, someone yelled. "Hey, Derby!"

Eliza looked around, expecting to see Sydney. Instead, Diana Wolanski was approaching, an amazingly friendly smile gracing her purple-lipsticked mouth.

"Eliza! I'm glad I spotted you away from the gang." Diana took a deep breath before continuing. "Look, I feel bad about the way I've been treating you and I'd like to make up for it. How about if we go ice-skating this afternoon—just us two girls? I drove to school today, so we can go in my car."

Eliza was dumbfounded. What miracle had taken place to change Diana's opinion of her?

"You look like you're in shock. Have I been that awful? Please forgive me and say you'll come skating with me," Diana said, speaking with unusual softness.

Eliza thought quickly. She couldn't possibly turn down this olive branch. Besides, she loved ice-skating. The only question was whether her mother would have a problem with a girl she'd never met driving her around. Then Eliza remembered. Wasn't Diana related to one of the Chamber of Commerce biggies her mother met with regularly?

"I'd love to go ice-skating. Let me just double check on something and I'll let you know for sure by lunchtime," Eliza said. She didn't want to reveal that she needed her mother's approval first.

A phone call to her mother was answered by voice mail, so she left a message saying she'd try back. As Eliza approached her locker later than usual, she searched for Sydney and, to her delight, found Joe waiting for her instead. There was just time to confirm their ice-skating date that Saturday before the bell rang. The school day proceeded at its normal uneven pace. Government with the dynamic and handsome Mr. Holland zoomed by, while history with the bored and boring Mrs. Fitzhue crawled slowly along.

Eliza managed to catch her mother just before lunch. There was, indeed, a Chamber of Commerce member with the last name of Wolanski and a teenage daughter. Since her mother was headed for a meeting with the general manager, the ice-skating venture with Diana was granted a hasty approval.

Finally, Eliza and Diana were enclosed together in Diana's car and headed for the ice-skating rink. Eliza began to have second thoughts about the whole undertaking. Diana hadn't spoken since mumbling a greeting outside the car and, surprisingly, she didn't turn the radio on. Eliza noticed that Diana seemed to be a decent driver, paying attention to traffic signs, using her turn signal and staying close to the speed limit.

They coasted to a stop at the busy intersection of Route 29 and Hydraulic Road and, since it was an extra-long traffic light, Eliza figured this was a good time to start a conversation. "Are you psyched about the trip to Washington, D.C.?" she asked.

Diana's shoulders jerked, shrugging off Eliza and her question, not even sparing her a glance. Their class would be going to Washington in a few weeks—in time for the cherry blossoms—and, until now, everyone Eliza had talked to was enthusiastic.

Eliza decided to try one more time. "Where do you get your hair cut? Mine needs a trim and I'd like to try somewhere new."

"Shear Power, but I don't think they do your kind of haircut," Diana said. This time she turned toward Eliza, running a flat, contemptuous glance over the long, straight, blunt-cut length of her hair.

The traffic light turned green, and Eliza was relieved to have Diana's attention return to the road. Diana had claimed that she wanted to make up for past behavior, yet she seemed more hostile than ever. Eliza sat in silent discomfort during the remainder of the drive.

By the time they walked into the Charlottesville Ice Park, Eliza was ready to call her mother and ask for a ride home, but the gleaming sheet of ice with its kaleidoscope of whirling figures beckoned. Light poured through glass doors and huge, Palladian-style windows into the high ceilinged room that served as both the reception and changing area.

As Eliza hesitated, taking in her surroundings, Diana strutted off toward the skate-rental booth. Eliza decided that since Diana was ignoring her, she'd return the favor. Just as she reached this decision, she heard a high peal of infectious laughter behind her and swung around. Devin and Derek were walking toward her, seemingly oblivious to her presence.

When the couple was within a few feet, Devin spotted her. Her mouth moved into a perfectly friendly smile, but Eliza sensed a lack of enthusiasm, which probably dated from their encounter at the movie theater. Eliza made a silent vow to avoid bringing up the murder.

"What are you doing—following us around?" Devin asked.

Eliza shook her head, not knowing how to respond. Devin's manner was light and joking, but Eliza sensed the underlying annoyance.

Derek bailed her out. "Charlottesville really is a small town. I'm always running into people I know."

"Let's hurry up and get our skates before there's a line," Devin said, gazing across the lobby to the entrance where a large group had just arrived.

Eliza was first to get her skates and, deciding to give Devin and Derek some space, she headed off immediately to one of the many heavy wooden benches. To her surprise, Devin and Derek followed and sat down beside her.

Devin finished putting on her skates first. "You have the loveliest sweaters. Is that one handmade?" she asked, gesturing toward Eliza's sweater.

Eliza was pleased that Devin was being so friendly. Struggling to get her left skate to fit as tightly as her right, she panted, "Yeah. It is. My mom found it when she went to Chicago last year."

Derek stood up, teetering slightly before catching his balance. "If you girls are finished chatting, let's hit the ice."

Devin wrinkled her nose in mock-annoyance and rose gracefully to her feet. Eliza gazed up at Derek, momentarily startled by how the skates emphasized his height and his broad-shouldered masculine strength. Then, having adjusted her left skate satisfactorily, she followed her companions.

Stepping onto the ice, Eliza felt an immediate heightening of her senses as brightly clad figures and lively music swirled around her. Soon, Devin, Derek and she were swept into the energy-charged whirl of color and sound. Eliza slowed her pace, deliberately separating herself from the couple. As she glided along, she gazed into the faces of passing skaters, hoping—and yet not hoping—to spot Diana. She would be shocked, but pleased, if Diana experienced a sudden change of heart and wanted to be friends.

A child of four or five years old dressed in a rainbow-striped pompom hat and cherry-red jacket clung tightly to her father with one hand and the rail with the other. To Eliza's astonishment, a tall girl with severely short hair held onto the rail a few feet behind the child, taking the same fearful baby steps. Diana behaved as if this were her first experience on the ice.

Eliza skated over to the rail. "You didn't tell me you'd never ice-skated before."

"You didn't ask," Diana said, but her tone lacked its usual tough edge.

"It won't take you long to catch on," Eliza said.

"Oh right! Have you been watching me at all?" Diana asked.

"Come on. Hold my hand and I'll show you," Eliza said with more confidence than she felt in showing Diana anything.

Still clutching the rail with one hand, Diana reached for Eliza with the other.

"Okay, now let go of the rail and push off with one foot, catch your balance and glide," Eliza said.

Diana pushed off timidly, teetering only slightly. As they circled the rink, she became braver. She pushed off strongly and Eliza, caught off guard, was dragged along with her. Eliza lost her balance and, before she knew it, she and Diana were sitting side-by-side on the ice. Eliza had to chuckle at the stunned look on Diana's face. She clambered to her feet, brushing off her sore and frozen rear-end before assisting Diana.

After the fall, Diana was braver. Perhaps falling was not as painful as she had imagined. Before long, she was taking short, stiff-legged glides across the ice on her own. She fell a couple more times, but each time resumed skating with increased determination. Eliza drifted away, wanting to stretch her legs in a fast-paced orbit of the rink. As she swooped around a group of people, she heard someone calling her name. She slowed her pace and Devin glided up beside her.

"Feels great, doesn't it?" Devin asked. Red-gold curls had escaped from her French twist, her eyes were incandescent amber and her cheeks glowed.

Eliza smiled and nodded, thinking it was no wonder that most of the men at the front desk were entranced by Devin and that Derek, too, seemed to be under her spell.

"I see you found a friend here," Devin commented.

"Actually, Diana and I came together," Eliza said, glancing around for Diana. A quick survey of the rink yielded no extremely tall, shorthaired girl. "I better find her; she's my ride home."

Eliza left Devin and skated over to the exit gate. She hobbled out to the lobby and peered toward the snack bar, thinking Diana might be taking a hot chocolate break. When she spotted Diana handing her skates in at the rental counter, she blinked in astonishment and headed over as quickly as possible.

"Diana!" she yelled, but the tall girl didn't even turn around. "Diana! Are you ready to leave?"

Diana turned toward her with a deadpan face, as if Eliza were a stranger—not the person who had helped her on the ice and certainly not a friend. "Why don't you catch a ride with your friends? I've got to go."

Eliza watched Diana stride off, standing there feeling helpless and foolish in her skates.

Chapter 14

Eliza would have to telephone her mother at the office. Her mother wouldn't be overjoyed to drive into town after a long day at work, but that would be more sensible than calling a taxi and less embarrassing than begging a ride from Devin and Derek. She turned around in search of a public telephone and there, as if by magic, stood Devin directly behind her.

"You look worried," Devin said.

Eliza could feel her smile wobble. "I'm okay. I just have to make a phone call. Have you seen a pay phone?"

"Come on, something's wrong. You look really upset," Devin said softly.

Hot tears prickled Eliza's eyelids but she refused to let them overflow. "I came with a friend, but she was mad at me or something and left without me."

Devin smiled and put an arm around Eliza's shoulders. "Well, I can fix that. Derek and I will give you a ride home."

"Sure. We'd be glad to," Derek said, coming up from behind them and causing Eliza to start.

"I live out in the county—close to the Silver Fox. I wouldn't want to take you out of your way," Eliza protested.

"It's no trouble at all," Derek said.

"Derek's going to think you don't like him if you won't accept a ride," Devin said with a teasing smile.

Eliza blushed. "Of course I like him, and I'd love a ride home. Thank you both for coming to my rescue."

Within twenty minutes, they were out of their ice-skates and walking toward the parking lot, heads bowed against a brisk and gusting wind. Although the wind was ripping at his clothing, Derek unlocked his hunter-green Ford Explorer and held the doors open with old-fashioned courtesy, first the front, passenger-side door for Devin then the back door for Eliza. It was nice to have the back seat to herself, Eliza thought, sinking into the soft leather seats and breathing in the new-car smell. When Derek joined the girls, he reached for Devin's hand and rested their entwined hands on the console between them. During the first few miles, Eliza was lulled into sleepiness by the gentle purr of the motor. The couple in front didn't turn on the radio or try to involve Eliza in conversation. Occasionally, they would murmur comments to one other.

After a while, Devin sat up and turned toward the back seat. "Derek's going to drop me off first."

"Okay," Eliza said, a little taken aback. What would she find to talk to Derek about? Silence might be awkward.

They pulled into a cul-de-sac of townhouses and parked in front of an end unit. It was too dark to see the neighborhood properly, but Eliza noticed patches of lawn and neatly-trimmed shrubbery in front of each residence and an abundance of trees in back. A porch light and a powerful lantern lit the front of Devin's brick home.

Derek walked around the Explorer and opened the door for Devin. Once again, Eliza was struck by his gentlemanly behavior.

"See you later, Eliza," Devin called as she stepped from the car.

Holding hands, Devin and Derek strolled up to the porch. Derek reached out to cup her upturned head in his hands and to kiss her lightly on the lips. He moved his hands to Devin's waist and one hand caught in her French twist—which had been threatening to fall down during the vigorous ice-skating session—causing it to finally give way. The wind gusted again, rippling Devin's cascade of red-gold curls and the scarf tied tightly at her throat.

Eliza felt the hairs rise on the back of her neck and all down her spine as she stared at the strawberry-blond curls, the scarf and a set of wide masculine shoulders. She barely noticed Devin's disappearance into the house. When Derek opened her door, she started in dismay.

"Why don't you sit up front with me so I don't feel like a chauffeur," he said.

Obediently, Eliza jumped out and climbed into the passenger-side front seat while Derek held the door open for her and shut it firmly behind her.

"I'm glad we have this little chance to talk," Derek said, glancing across the car's dusky interior before turning the ignition.

While he put the car into reverse, Eliza stared straight ahead reassuring herself that it was the shadows that had made his face look menacing. But what could they possibly have to talk about?

As soon as Derek exited the cul-de-sac, he began speaking in a low, intense voice. "Someone that works with Devin told me what you've been up to and I want it to stop."

"Wha—" Eliza began, but she was cut off.

"And don't put on the innocent act. I might have fallen for it once—at the movie theater—but I won't make that mistake again. You know very well what I'm talking about. All your endless questions about the murder—which seem to point in one direction—establishing Devin's or my guilt. You pretend to be Devin's friend while you encourage her to spill her guts about her friendship with Fiona. And, if that wasn't enough, the day after I met you at the theater, I had a little visit from Detective Thompson. Guess what he wanted to know? My whereabouts on Friday, February 26!

"You're making my life miserable while you play at being a detective. I live in the grown-up world, little girl. I've got to make it as a builder in this town, and, with all the competition here, it isn't easy. I'm relying on my reputation and contacts. The last thing I need is some punk kid getting in my way," Derek said in what had become a deep-throated growl.

"But I haven't spoken to Detective Thompson," Eliza protested, finally waking from her shock enough to defend herself.

Derek smirked. "Yeah, right."

Although stung by his calling her 'little girl' and 'punk kid' and by his unjust accusations, Eliza had been, until now, cowed by his anger. Then the look on his face and his derisive sarcasm triggered a molten heat that swept through her body like lava through a volcano. She could feel herself shaking with the effort to hold it in. She had one more pointed question to ask, and anger had driven away her fear of asking it.

"What were you and Fiona arguing about a couple days before her murder?" Eliza demanded, her voice sounding loud and surprisingly steady in her own ears.

The Explorer had been zipping along at a good rate of speed when it made a sudden swerve onto the shoulder. Eliza grabbed the dashboard. Her head whipped forward then backward as the car jerked to an abrupt stop, tires squealing. Her heart pumped furiously. As she withdrew shaking hands from the dashboard, she glanced across the semi-darkness to another pair of hands still gripping the steering wheel. Her eyes traveled up to Derek's face and met a white-hot glare that managed to penetrate the vehicle's murky interior. As she rubbed her sore neck, she sensed that nothing would give him more pleasure than shaking her until she truly had whiplash.

Derek reached out and Eliza flinched, but he was only switching on the overhead light. A detached part of Eliza's mind noted just how strikingly-handsome and boyishly-endearing Derek's features were and just how menacing.

"Fiona started the argument," Derek began in a low, rasping voice. "She had the gall to accuse Devin of keeping a piece of borrowed jewelry. Naturally, Devin had already returned the jewelry, but Fiona had so much stuff she lost track. When she brought it up with me, I gave her something to think about. I told her what a sorry friend she was."

Then he leaned toward Eliza, pointing his forefinger at her and raising his voice. "Just like I'm telling you. Quit taking advantage of Devin's sweet nature. Stop asking your stupid questions and stay away from her—and me—from now on!" By the time he reached the last sentence, he was shouting, his face beet-red and convulsed with rage.

Eliza nodded numbly. She had no intention of going near him after this. She couldn't speak past her fear-frozen throat muscles. If she were capable of speaking, he wouldn't listen anyway.

Derek jerked the handle on the steering column into drive and pulled back onto the road, resuming his previous pace. She gazed out the passenger-side window, avoiding the smallest glimpse of him. Even if it had not been a gloomy, star-less night—she wouldn't have noticed the scenery outside the window. Her mind flashed with images as if a disjointed home movie were running inside her head. The brassy young waitress telling her how Fiona seemed quite taken with her lunch companion. Red-gold curls lying against a dark sleeve. A tall man with powerful shoulders holding a woman in his arms.

Derek's angry, distorted features. A scarf tied around a woman's throat... The scarf—Fiona had worn a scarf! Eliza returned to reality with a start. Now she had a reason to see Detective Thompson.

She worked up the courage to glance at her companion. It occurred to her that he hadn't asked for directions. They'd passed the inn a short way back, so he was headed in the right direction, but what if he didn't intend to take her home?

He must have sensed her gaze. "Devin told me where you live, but it's so dark out here you'll have to tell me where to turn."

"Okay," Eliza said, her voice cracking with relief. "Turn right where the white fencing ends. We live in the cottage a little ways past the main house."

When he pulled up in front of the cottage, she didn't give him a chance to open the door for her. "Thanks!" she yelled, unworried about how idiotic that sounded after the way he'd treated her. She sprinted up the front steps of the house, not looking back until the front door was shut behind her and the deadbolt securely turned in the lock. She watched the Explorer's tail lights until they disappeared into the night.

Chapter 15

"What are you doing here? Why aren't you at school?" Jordan asked, loudly.

Eliza flinched. These were the questions she had been avoiding all morning. She had left the cottage, as usual, supposedly headed for the bus stop at the farm entrance. When the bus approached, she had hidden behind a tree, and it didn't even slow down. After her mother drove past, the coast was clear, and she stepped out of hiding and struck off along the road toward the Silver Fox.

Again, Eliza had avoided confiding in her mother. Fiona Dulaney had been killed practically before her very eyes and she had been too dense to understand what was happening. Now, she knew there were contributions she could make toward finding the murderer, and she was afraid her mother would interfere. Derek's menacing behavior had frightened her last night, but, in the bright light of day, his conduct made her all the more determined. She was being taken seriously by at least one person. She would simply have to be more discreet.

Now, on her way to enlist Wanda's assistance, she had been spotted by Jordan. Although he would be harder to convince, perhaps he could help her instead. Eliza made a quick assessment of the situation at the front desk. Devin was on the switchboard and the new clerk, Harry, was seated in front of a computer terminal. This meant that, if Jordan were cooperative, he could leave the two, more 'junior' clerks in charge of the desk briefly while he attended to business elsewhere.

As he crossed the room toward Eliza, Jordan raised an expressive eyebrow. Eliza pointed meaningfully toward the conference room door. He rolled his eyes, before following Eliza into the conference room. She locked the door carefully behind him.

"This better be good," he said.

"It is. First, I have to tell you something Detective Thompson told me to keep to myself. Promise you won't repeat it."

Jordan rolled his eyes again. "I promise. You're being a little theatrical, you know. I thought that was my department."

Eliza sighed. When would people take her seriously? Then she began to speak in a deliberately lowered tone. "Late in the afternoon—the afternoon Fiona was killed—I inadvertently opened the door to her hotel room and saw a man embracing her. No one saw me—the man's back was turned toward me, and he blocked Fiona's view of me. I left as quickly and quietly as possible."

When Jordan began shaking his head in an admonitory way, Eliza rushed ahead before he could interrupt. "Forget my actions. The point is: I saw Fiona shortly before she was killed. I may have been a partial witness to her murder. I described everything to the police except for something I remembered last night. Could you take me to the police station so that I can tell them about it?"

Jordan held up the palms of his hands. "Who-o-oa! You've hit me with a lot here. You're telling me that you might have been the last person—other than Fiona's killer—to see her alive!"

"Keep your voice down!" Eliza hissed. "Will you take me to the police station or not?"

Jordan crossed his arms over his chest. "I need more information first. What are you planning to tell the police?"

Eliza took a deep breath. "Well, it's complicated. Do you want the short version or the long version?"

Jordan pulled out a couple of the conference table chairs and waved her into one of them. He straddled the other himself, arms resting along the back of the chair and cat-like, hazel eyes watching her intently. "Better give me the whole story."

Eliza explained how she'd gone ice-skating the day before with Diana and ended up leaving with Devin and Derek. She described the déjà vu-like tableaux when Derek had embraced Devin. The wind had swept Devin's scarf into motion, triggering Eliza's memory of the scarf Fiona had worn on the evening of her murder.

"Derek is built just like the man I saw holding Fiona," Eliza said. "Plus, he was so angry last night, it was scary. Afterwards, I was kind of suspicious. Either he has an unbelievably bad temper or he has something to hide."

"You know the whole ice-skating thing sounds like a set-up to me. You just happen to end up alone in Derek's car so that he can drill you about minding your own business?" Jordan's eyebrow inched toward his hairline.

Eliza's hands rose to her mouth. "You're right. I never thought of that... Maybe Derek asked Diana to bring me to the rink so that I would end up going home with him. Except—how would they know each other?"

"Maybe they don't. Maybe Devin knows Diana," Jordan said.

Eliza frowned. "Devin wouldn't have set me up like that. Besides it was Derek who grilled me. Devin wasn't even there when he turned mean. And, there's something else you don't know. Derek was seen having a heated argument with Fiona just a couple days before she was killed."

Jordan's forehead crinkled in thought, his beautifully curved mouth drooping downwards for several moments before he spoke. "Let's forget about Derek for a moment and concentrate on the scarf. What if the scarf was used to strangle Fiona?"

Eliza's chest tightened. "It was just this gauzy, yellow material—you know, kind of see-through. It doesn't seem like it would be substantial enough—"

Jordan's hazel eyes narrowed. "Hold on. Describe this scarf for me—in detail."

Eliza was puzzled. "I told you. It was yellow and gauzy. Plus, there were these pink splotches..."

Jordan spun around in his chair and shot to his feet. He unbuttoned his jacket and stuck his hand inside. He tugged gently and soon a long rectangle of gossamer-thin, yellow material hung from his fingertips. The scarf was dotted with bright-fuchsia flowers.

"Does this look familiar?" Jordan asked.

Eliza felt the hairs rising on the back of her neck. "Th-that's her scarf. How did you get it?"

The obvious answer popped into her head, and, eyes widening with horror, she gazed at the tall, wide-shouldered man standing before her.

Jordan raised his palms. "Don't even go there. You know me better than that."

Immediately, Eliza was stricken with remorse. Jordan was no killer. She could recall many instances in which Jordan had demonstrated remarkable kindness.

"I'm sorry. As soon as I had time to think, I knew it wasn't true," Eliza said, contritely.

"You bet! If the killer was white, my hair's all wrong," Jordan said with a grin, hazel eyes glinting devilishly.

Eliza looked at his tight, black hair, cheeks flaming. "That's not how I knew it couldn't be you—"

Jordan interrupted, his mobile features growing serious. "The point is—are you sure this is Fiona's scarf?"

Eliza nodded. "Ninety-nine percent sure. Where did you find it?"

"Right here," Jordan said, pulling back his jacket lapel to reveal an inside breast pocket. He folded the scarf neatly and tucked it carefully back into its original resting place, before continuing. "Yesterday afternoon on the way out of here, I picked up my dry cleaning as usual. Then, this morning I realized I had the wrong jacket. I looked at the dry cleaning ticket, and, sure enough, I'd been given Johnny's jacket. I guess Johnny Burnett and Jordan Blake look pretty similar scribbled on a dry cleaning ticket. Since I need to be in uniform and Johnny and I are the same size, I wore his jacket. Here—I'll show you something else."

Jordan shrugged off the jacket, and displayed the label sewn into the lining—J.L.B.

Eliza frowned. "But this makes no sense. Johnny couldn't be the killer. It must be Derek..."

"Let's not try to figure this out on our own. We've got to go see Detective Thompson—now," Jordan said, his voice urgent.

Eliza nodded. "You're right."

Jordan informed Devin and the new clerk that an emergency had come up, requiring his departure. Robert Avery wasn't on duty and Jordan didn't bother seeking the assistant manager's approval. He did insist, however, on going by the sales department on the way out and informing Eliza's mother of their plans. Eliza was relieved to learn that her mother was in a meeting with the general manager. Instead of explaining her misadventures to her mother, Eliza simply wrote a note and left it on her mother's desk.

Eliza and Jordan raced from the sales office to the employee parking lot and jumped into Jordan's 1970's-era Lincoln Town Car. Although Eliza experienced a twinge of concern about the enormous car's rusty-silver, paint-chipped exterior—the plush, leather interior and the smooth roar of the engine restored her confidence. With Jordan sliding through yellow lights and zipping past vehicles on the 250 bypass and with Eliza hanging onto the dashboard, they made it to the Albemarle County office building on McIntire Road in record time.

The police department, along with the other county departments, was housed in a handsome, sprawling, red-brick building that had once been the city of Charlottesville's high school. Jordan drove into the north-side parking lot and pulled up between two white Crown Victorias. As Eliza approached the station entrance with Jordan by her side, the reality of what she was doing sunk in for the first time. Her legs were weak and her palms were sweaty—the way they'd been a couple months ago when she'd had to make a ten-minute oral presentation. She glanced up at Jordan's face and read only determination on his dark, handsome features.

Upon entering the building, Eliza and Jordan headed directly to the reception desk.

A tall man with a long, basset hound face looked up from some papers he was working on. "Hi, folks. How can I help you?" he asked, his eyes sweeping over Eliza and settling upon Jordan.

Eliza lifted her chin. "We'd like to see Detective David Thompson. We have some information about the Dulaney murder."

For half a second, the officer's droopy eyes were startled into some semblance of wakefulness. Then he asked their names, announced their presence and, within minutes, they were being escorted to homicide.

They walked down a snaking corridor and through a room filled with rows of mostly empty desks before being led into a small, cramped office.

Detective Thompson unfolded his long length from behind the desk, looking more stately than ever in a crisp, charcoal suit. He waved them into the seats in front of him and sat back down. "Would either of you like a soft drink?"

Officer Lewis detached himself from the wall where he was leaning then settled back to his original spot as Jordan and Eliza declined. For her part, Eliza was eager to divulge her story—beginning with the scarf.

"I've remembered something else about the day Fiona was killed," Eliza said. "Yesterday, Derek Russell gave me a ride home from the ice-skating rink. He dropped his girlfriend—Devin Cooper—off first. When he kissed her good night, I got this spooky feeling of déjà vu. It was as if I were standing in the doorway of Fiona's guest room, once again, staring at a tall, big-shouldered guy holding Fiona, so that all I could see of her was this long strand of strawberry-blond hair. Only this time, the wind was blowing her hair and scarf all over the place. And that's when it hit me. On the day she was killed, Fiona was wearing a scarf—a yellow scarf with pink flowers made out of this gauzy, see-through material."

Despite his distinguished appearance, Detective Thompson's deep-set eyes were so shadowed they appeared sunken, and permanent lines scored his forehead and cheeks, making him look sad and exhausted. However, at the mention of the scarf, he sat forward alertly, pinpointing Eliza with faded-blue eyes which seemed to possess the powers of a cat scan. She was grateful when Jordan cleared his throat, drawing the detective's gaze away from her.

"Eliza needed a ride to the police station, sir," Jordan said.

"When I insisted on an explanation and she told me about the scarf, I was floored. You see, last night the dry cleaners at the inn gave me the wrong jacket, but I didn't know until I was dressing for work this morning. Then, I found Johnny's initials in the jacket lining and realized that the dry cleaners had misread the ticket, confusing Jordan Blake and Johnny Burnett.

"Now—this is the critical part. When I was studying the lining, I noticed that there was something in the inside pocket. It turned out to be a yellow scarf, sir. According to Eliza, the scarf belongs—belonged to Miss Dulaney." As he finished up his story, Jordan peeled off the jacket he was still wearing and laid it neatly upon Detective Thompson's desk, explaining that the scarf was now where he'd originally found it—in the jacket's inside pocket.

Officer Lewis sprang from his leaning post against the wall and stood hovering by the desk.

Detective Thompson pulled on a pair of latex gloves and extracted the scarf, dangling it from his long fingers like a flag. He studied the length and breadth of it closely for several moments, before inserting the scarf into a plastic evidence bag.

"I'm afraid we'll have to hold onto the scarf and the jacket. Now, Jordan, think about this a moment before you answer. Since the scarf has been in your possession, has anyone else handled it or even touched it?"

Jordan shook his head emphatically. "No. Eliza's the only one who even knows about the scarf."

A smile softened David Thompson's somber features. "You two did terrific work! Finding this scarf may turn out to be a critical part of our investigation."

This was dismissal, but Eliza had more to say. "Are you going to arrest Johnny Burnett?" she asked.

"Perhaps, but we have work to do first," the detective replied noncommittally.

He stood up as if preparing to usher them out, his giant body making the room seem closet-sized. Jordan rose respectfully.

"There are a couple other things you might want to hear," Eliza said, remaining seated.

Detective Thompson sank back down into his chair and Jordan followed suit. "All right, young lady. What else do you have for me?"

Eliza could sense that beneath the detective's unreadable features and calm demeanor, he was frustrated by this delay. His internal engine was humming at full throttle, eager for action, and Eliza was forcing him to stop and listen. She would try to be concise.

"There are three events I want to describe," she began and she explained how she'd been locked in the meat freezer, how her favorite jump had been rigged with wire to cause a fall and how scary and threatening Derek Russell had been the night he gave her a ride home.

"Derek was angry with me to begin with, but his temper shot right through the roof when I asked him about his argument with Fiona," Eliza remarked.

The permanent lines across Detective Thompson's forehead became furrows, so she hastily backtracked. "You see, Franky—one of the food and beverage set-up guys—saw Derek and Fiona having a serious argument a couple days before she was killed. Franky wasn't close enough to make out their actual words, so I was dying to know what the argument was about."

"Haven't you ever heard the expression 'Curiosity killed the cat'?" Jordan asked.

Eliza ignored him, keeping her eyes on the detective. "When I asked Derek about the argument, he pulled the car off the road and just lost it. He began ranting about how Fiona had accused Devin of keeping some jewelry she'd borrowed. Then Derek started yelling at me, telling me to leave Devin and him alone and stop asking questions about the murder. He was really psycho."

Eliza tried to gauge Detective Thompson's reaction, but his face was quite inscrutable. "I would have told you all this sooner, but I wanted to have something concrete..."

David Thompson leaned across the desk. "Don't wait until you have something big. Next time, if there is a next time, let me or my office know about even the smallest thing as soon as it occurs. Otherwise, you could put yourself in danger and slow down the investigation. Do I have your promise?"

Feeling chastened, Eliza nodded. "Yes."

Once again, he rose from his chair and, this time, Eliza followed his example meekly. As the station doors closed behind Jordan and her, the same questions kept revolving through her mind. Whom did the police suspect now that they had Eliza's information? What action would they take now that Fiona Dulaney's scarf was in their possession?

Chapter 16

Eliza had to wait until the following day before receiving the answers to her questions. After school, she was walking toward the bus when someone called her name. She looked around and, to her amazement, there was an enormous, silver Lincoln Town Car idling next to a school bus.

Eliza ran over to the driver's-side window. "Don't you know they only allow buses back here?"

Jordan made a face. "Climb in and I'll rectify the situation."

Eliza ran around the car's long hood and jumped in beside him, hurling her backpack into the back seat. "What're you doing here?"

"Is that the thanks I get for doing you a favor on my day off?" Jordan asked.

He backed up and headed out of the bus area. Eliza leaned back in her seat, gazing out her window at the curious students staring at the big Lincoln, its handsome driver and Eliza as they passed by. She was proud to be seen with Jordan, yet felt kind of silly about her own reaction. His dignity and self-confidence could be read in his dark profile. He was naturally charismatic, naturally cool.

As they were coasting along behind a line of cars leaving the school parking lot, Jordan glanced over at her. "The police arrested Johnny Burnett. I thought you'd want to know as soon as possible."

As soon as she'd spotted Jordan's car, Eliza had suspected as much. What else would be momentous enough to bring

Jordan to Albemarle High to pick her up? She was quiet a moment, trying to figure out why she felt so unsettled by the news.

Jordan raised an eyebrow. "I thought you'd be happy that the killer had been caught, and you helped make it happen."

"Thanks for coming to tell me," she said. "All day I've been wondering whether they'd arrest him, but now that they have, it doesn't seem real. Johnny—a murderer? He doesn't have enough feeling about anything—except maybe his family pedigree and his fancy car—to commit murder. Plus, why would he kill Fiona Dulaney? I don't see the connection."

Jordan shrugged with cat-like grace. "Beats me, but that scarf was pretty incriminating."

"Not if someone was trying to implicate Johnny by planting the scarf in his jacket pocket," Eliza said, her voice rising with excitement.

"Hold it, hold on. Unlike some of us poor slobs—who don't care how we look when we're out of view answering the switchboard or whatever—Johnny never removes his jacket when he's working. It would take an invisible man to slip that scarf into Johnny's pocket between the time he took off his jacket and when he handed it directly to the dry-cleaning clerk," Jordan pointed out.

Eliza frowned. "I just don't get it."

By the time Jordan pulled up in front of the inn, Eliza still hadn't come up with a likely motive for Johnny Burnett. As she waved to Jordan from the curb, she tried to put thoughts of the murder aside. The killer had been found, and she had a lengthy algebra assignment to get through. Then again, she hadn't spoken to Wanda lately. What would Wanda make of Johnny's arrest? Maybe she could provide some insight into his criminal tendencies.

Wanda was hanging up the phone as Eliza entered the food and beverage office. Her eyes were round with excitement, her plump cheeks, cherry-red.

"Guess you've heard the news," Eliza said.

"Yeah. Johnny was arrested this morning. Johnny Burnett—amazing," Wanda said. Then she added in a knowing tone, "But maybe it's not so amazing when you know the family history."

"What history?" Eliza asked.

"Well, Johnny's father was kind of the black sheep of the Dulaney family. Only he wasn't actually a Dulaney. He was married to Fiona Dulaney's aunt."

Eliza digested this. "Which means Fiona and Johnny are—were—cousins."

She felt a stab of annoyance with herself for not making the connection before this. Just a few days ago, Joe McClellan had talked about how Fiona's aunt and her family lived at the Dulaney estate. Joe had been referring to Johnny's mother. Johnny had been raised in an opulent house without the money to match his surroundings and with a drug addict for a father.

"Still, why would Johnny kill his cousin?" she asked, speaking her next thought aloud.

"Jealousy, plain and simple," Wanda stated. "You see, after Fiona's grandfather died, Fiona's father received the estate, and the rest of her grandfather's assets were divided pretty evenly between her father and her aunt. Now, Fiona's father invested his money wisely and made a pile of money, whereas Fiona's aunt married a druggie and her inheritance was squandered. When Fiona was about five years old, her mother died and she and her father moved away from Charlottesville. By that time, her aunt's family were in pretty desperate shape, so Fiona's father let them live at the family estate—though it still belonged to him."

Eliza's brow creased. "You'd think that Johnny would have been grateful to his uncle."

"Charity often inspires resentment, not gratitude. Johnny must have been more resentful than most," Wanda said. Her feverish excitement was replaced by a distant sagacity giving her the look of a wise cherub.

Eliza chewed at her lower lip. "Okay, but murder is so extreme—so evil. What drove Johnny to such lengths and why now?"

Wanda shrugged. "Maybe we'll find out eventually."

Eliza frowned. She wanted the motivation for this murder to be as neatly tied together as the killer's motivation always was in one of the Kinsey Millhone mysteries. There were so many loose ends. Maybe Wanda could help her with one of them.

"There's another thing that's bugging me. Have you ever heard of a girl named Diana Wolanski? And, if so, what possible connection could she have with Devin's boyfriend, Derek Russell?"

Wanda's round eyes grew even rounder. "Huh? Why don't you try filling those questions in with a little background."

Eliza explained how Diana had invited her to go ice-skating, only to abandon her, forcing her to accept a ride with Derek. He had taken the opportunity to deliver a diatribe about how she was ruining his career as a builder and about how she was taking advantage of Devin's sweet nature.

"Do you think Diana and Derek were in cahoots?" asked Eliza.

Wanda's face assumed the wise-cherub expression once again. "They must have been. Think about it. She asks you to go ice-skating with her, then acts hostile. Once there, it's obvious she's never skated, so you help her out and she's friendlier.

Next thing you know, she ditches you. Could anything be more schizoid?"

"But how could Diana Wolanski and Derek know each other? What's the connection?" Eliza asked.

Wanda's forehead creased. "Wolanski... Tom Wolanski is a hotshot builder. He's developed half a dozen subdivisions all over town, and he's very involved with the Chamber of Commerce. Is Diana any relation?"

"I think she's his daughter," Eliza said slowly. "If Tom Wolanski's a builder and Derek's a builder, they might know each other. Then, Derek could have easily met Diana."

Wanda grinned, dimples flashing. "There you have it!"

Eliza hugged Wanda's cushiony little body. "Thanks, partner. Another mystery solved!"

Of course, there was no way of knowing what really happened without getting a truthful answer from the parties involved. Knowing Derek and Diana's attitude toward her, that wasn't about to happen. Still, talking to Wanda was so reassuring.

Her mood considerably lighter, Eliza headed to the conference room and her homework. She pulled out her algebra book, notebook paper and two freshly sharpened pencils, but the algebra problems dissolved before her eyes and were replaced by Derek's angry, snarling countenance. She had been so sure he was Fiona's killer. Could the police be wrong?

The door cracked open and Devin's lovely face appeared. "I've got spring fever. Want to go up on the roof with me before my shift begins?"

Eliza jumped up from the table. Although Derek had ordered her to stay away from him and Devin—obviously, he had not consulted Devin first. Eliza refused to let his threats break up her friendship with Devin.

While roughly two-thirds of the inn possessed an ordinary gable roof, the remaining third had a flat-topped roof and parapet. During the late spring and summer, outdoor furniture was set up, and the flat-topped roof became a favorite gathering spot. Eliza hadn't been up there in months. Besides, some fresh air would clear her tangled thoughts so that she could concentrate on her homework.

The sun poured down from a cloudless, still sky, making the cool, spring day refreshing rather than chilly. Eliza followed Devin over the rooftop's damp surface, avoiding the puddles formed from melted ice, until they reached the edge. The rolling grounds of the Inn below were lovely, even cloaked in winter's drab colors. The mountains—though miles away—seemed breathtakingly close, as if they could be reached by crossing the very next rise.

"Are you going to the figure-skating show this weekend?" Devin asked.

Eliza shook her head. "No. At least, I hadn't planned to. What kind of show is it?"

"They're doing a spring festival theme to raise money for charity. There'll be a couple of Olympic stars and lots of wannabees. It should be fun," Devin explained.

Eliza watched a hawk, wings outstretched, riding the air currents. There were always plenty of buzzards around, not many hawks. The hawk took a sudden dive, and she imagined a small creature below, going about its business, all unknowing.

She gazed up at her friend, captured for a moment by her unearthly beauty. The sun had turned Devin's hair to fire and caused her amber eyes to sparkle and her flawless skin to glow.

Eyes smarting from the strong sunlight and Devin's bright visage, Eliza glanced downwards and found herself reeling from a sudden sense of vertigo. When Devin's hands settled lightly upon her shoulders, she started and, to her horror, began to slide. Her arms flailed in a desperate attempt to regain her balance, while she envisioned toppling over the parapet to the flagstones two stories below.

"Miss Cooper! Miss Cooper!" a masculine voice shouted.

Devin's hands steadied Eliza, keeping her upright.

"That must be Robert, but my shift doesn't begin for another twenty minutes," Devin said, her voice oddly harsh.

Shakily, Eliza turned and saw two uniformed figures striding rapidly in their direction. "It's the police," she said, her voice rising in surprise.

Her surprise changed to astonishment when a slap-slapping noise filled her ears, and, turning back, she watched Devin race across the wet rooftop, heading toward the fire escape ladder, long legs flashing. She didn't get far. The two officers broke into a run, and the female officer—younger than her partner and a lithe six feet or more—brought Devin down with a flying tackle. Seconds later, her stocky, beefy-shouldered counterpart caught up and helped Devin to her feet and into a pair of handcuffs.

Meanwhile, the female officer began reciting the words made familiar by television shows involving law enforcement: 'You have the right to remain silent...'

Devin's eyes were huge and frightened, her mouth trembled, tendrils of strawberry-blond hair curled wildly on either side of her face, her blouse was untucked and her skirt splattered with dirty water. She was speaking in a high-pitched voice, while her escorts watched, flat-eyed. Meanwhile, Eliza had crept toward the others until she was just a few feet away, hoping to intervene on Devin's behalf if possible.

"Why are you arresting me? If Johnny told you I had something to do with Fiona's death, he's lying," Devin said.

"We've searched your place, Miss Cooper," the female officer stated.

Devin hunched her shoulders and crossed her arms, self-protectively. "Well, you would have found the jewelry I borrowed. That's no crime. We were best friends for God's sake. She was always lending me stuff."

"Including uncut gems, Miss Cooper? And, since you had nothing to hide, why were you running away from us?" the female officer asked, sarcastically.

Devin gazed at the male officer with a child's wide-eyed innocence, as if he were the one inquiring. "It was just pure instinct. You all looked so grim—so purposeful, I was frightened. As for the jewels, Johnny must have planted them."

The female officer rolled her eyes. "Now why would he do that? He'd already confessed to first-degree murder. He had no motive for implicating you," she said. "Unless it was his sense of justice."

"You bitch!" Devin cried sharply. She directed a hurt, limpid gaze at the male officer, once again, and spoke softly. "Can you believe she said that to me? Johnny had a serious crush on me. He kept asking me out and I kept turning him down. He became bitter—but I had no idea he was angry enough to implicate me in Fiona's murder."

"Give it up, Miss Cooper," the male officer said, his voice like steel. "Johnny wasn't mad at you, just like he's not mad at you now. As soon as we frightened him into telling us where the jewels were, he tried to take back his words and steer us in another direction. Tried to say it was all Derek Russell's doing, but that wouldn't fly. What I want to know is—why did you seduce Johnny Burnett into killing your best friend? Were the jewels worth it?"

Devin squared her drooping shoulders, and her mantle of

injured innocence fell away. Moments before her lips had trembled; now they formed a self-satisfied smirk. "Johnny would have done anything for me. Besides, he'd had enough of Fiona and her father's charity. He was tired of endless comparisons to his perfect little cousin. Fiona never lifted a finger to get what she wanted. She was just born to it."

Eliza watched Devin's face in dismay. The older girl's bow-shaped lips drew back from her teeth in a snarl, and her eyes, lovely only minutes before, glazed over with hatred—cutting off the light.

"Fiona only thought she was my best friend. She was more like my best enemy," Devin spat. "She was after Derek—even though she knew I was crazy about him. Just imagine—this girl had everything her heart desired, but it was not enough. She tried to take Derek from me—to tell him ugly lies about me so he'd be free to go to her. What kind of friend lends you her jewelry, then accuses you of stealing and pawning it? If she'd continued to drip her poison, Fiona might have convinced Derek. He's terribly ambitious. With Fiona's money and family position, nothing could have stopped him.

"But, he wouldn't have been happy," Devin stated, shaking her head with conviction. "He wouldn't have loved her like he loves me. Something had to be done. When Fiona showed me the collection of jewelry and gems she recklessly kept in her room at the inn, I knew the time was right. With a little persuading, Johnny agreed to help. We had to get rid of Fiona. Once she vanished from our lives, Johnny would be his wealthy uncle's heir and I would have Derek and the jewels."

Devin swung toward Eliza, eyes opaque with hatred. "I didn't believe anyone would pay attention to your childish snooping. Johnny warned me, but I wouldn't listen—until they dragged him off to jail. You're just lucky the police got here when they did."

"That's enough, Miss Cooper," the male officer growled, yanking Devin into action. He and his partner led Devin away, one on either side of her like brown bookends.

Eliza stood rooted to the spot. The events of the last several minutes were so unexpected, so contrary to her view of reality, she felt lost. She forced herself to move, to go back to the place where she'd nearly fallen, to look down. As she suspected, there was ice—a narrow band rimming the base of the parapet, protected by its shadow. Had Devin known about the ice, luring her up to the rooftop in order to stage an 'accidental' fall? Would Devin have prevented that fall if there had been no shouts? Although Eliza would never know for certain, she had no doubt about the crucial, underlying point.

Devin was a killer. She might not have been physically present when Fiona struggled for her last breath, but she was there in hate-filled spirit. Devin's eerily transformed face and ugly words reverberated through Eliza's mind, as they would for a long time to come.

Chapter 17

While students teemed about her with their usual boisterous energy, Eliza moved toward her locker as if she were an automaton. Sydney straightened up from her leaning post against the lockers, her face lighting up with that sweet, pearly smile. Eliza's mood lifted slightly until she noticed what Sydney was wearing. Sydney's bright turquoise turtleneck and black jeans were cinched by a black belt with a silver buckle. Eliza's spirits plummeted once again.

"Hey, you look like you just lost your best friend," Sydney said.

Eliza's mind seized on the words 'best friend' and flashed to the scene yesterday. Fiona had thought Devin was her best friend—a sister.

Sydney was waving a hand in front of Eliza's face. "Earth to Eliza. Do you read me? Come in, Eliza."

A spurt of anger pierced Eliza's dullness. "Hey, Sydney. Nice belt. Where'd you get it?"

"Thanks," Sydney said, ignoring the question. "Come on. You sure are slow this mornin'. The gang's probably wonderin' where we are."

Eliza began dialing the combination to her locker, hands shaky on the cold metal. "You go ahead. I'm going to pass."

Sydney stared at Eliza for a full minute, while her surprised expression darkened to sulky displeasure. "Okay. You sure are in a strange mood this mornin'. Let me know when you're feelin' like yourself again."

Eliza watched Sydney stalk off, one of the best-dressed girls at Albemarle High and one of the prettiest with her honey-blond hair and perfect smile. Although there was a lump in her throat, Eliza knew she had done the right thing.

As she gathered her books and papers and turned from her locker, she saw Joe McClellan approaching. The serious girl from the newspaper staff strode by his side, and the fact that she was three inches taller seemed not to worry Joe in the least. He cut over to Eliza, while the girl kept on walking, giving Joe a wave and smiling at Eliza, braces glinting, as she passed. Even in her somber mood, Eliza found herself responding to the warmth of that smile. *Braces or no braces, Joe's friend should smile more often*, she thought.

"How are you?" Joe asked.

"Okay," Eliza said, huskily.

Joe frowned. "Really okay?" He reached out and brushed a strand of hair out of her face and his hand lingered for a moment, as gentle and shivery as a whisper against her cheek.

Eliza nodded. "It's been a tough couple of days. They found the killers."

Joe's eyes widened. "Killers, as in more than one?"

"Yeah. It's a long story," Eliza said. "Let's find a private place to talk, and I'll tell you about it."

They walked to the same empty classroom they'd found that first morning. Joe shoved two adjacent desks together in the far corner of the room, and they sat down. Keeping her voice low, Eliza related the events of the past few days while he listened intently.

As she told her story, Eliza went through—in fast forward—the gamut of emotions she'd experienced when the events took place. By the time she finished talking, she felt exhausted. "You know, I thought I had it figured out, but boy was I ever wrong.

There were just all these hidden agendas I knew nothing about."

Joe shook his head in amazement. "I would have suspected Derek Russell, too, after the way he treated you. Then Jordan found the scarf in Johnny's pocket, pointing you in a totally different direction. And—talk about hidden agendas—the whole scene with Devin just blows my mind! One moment she was a really nice girl and the next moment she turned into this hate-filled witch."

"She didn't turn into someone else," Eliza said. "She just removed the lovely, sweet-tempered mask she wore and all her pent-up hatred poured out."

"There's one other thing I don't understand. Who locked you in the meat freezer and who rigged your favorite jump with wire?" Joe asked.

Eliza shrugged. "Johnny, probably. Devin mentioned that he was worried about her letting her guard down around me. Plus, you should have seen how freaky he acted one day when I was talking to Devin about Fiona. He banged things around and stormed off without saying a word. That was the same day I got locked in the freezer."

Joe frowned. "You know, Johnny was clearly unstable. Still, Devin must have been a hypnotist to get him to commit murder."

Eliza shook her head. "It's true that he idolized her, but, when it came to Fiona, Devin was just feeding his hatred with her own. They both were so consumed with envy that they began to see Fiona as a completely worthless person. By the time they plotted her death, they had convinced themselves that she deserved to die. Two people with the same distorted view of reality. It's scary."

"The final straw for Devin must have been the threat of losing Derek," Joe said.

"Yeah. It seems to have pushed her over the edge," Eliza

agreed. "The worst thing is, judging by what Derek said to me when he drove me home, he had zero interest in Fiona. You know, he was kind of old-fashioned toward Devin. It was as if he was a knight in shining armor and he'd sworn an oath of honor to protect this helpless, innocent damsel in distress. He was loyal and protective and totally convinced that Fiona was making false accusations."

Joe was silent for several moments. "Hatred is blinding. After a while, Devin and Johnny couldn't see the truth anymore, only what their hatred led them to believe," he said slowly.

"Fiona was killed, and it was all for nothing," Eliza said.

Their desks formed one, long bench interrupted only by an iron desktop bracket. Joe put an arm around her. Eliza leaned toward him and rested there—her head cradled in the crook of his neck and shoulder. She closed her eyes, ignoring the pinch of the metal bracket at her ribcage and concentrating on a reassuring mixture of sensations—the soft, cotton shirt beneath her cheek; the familiar, faint scent of horses and the heavy warmth of his strong arm about her.

After a couple minutes, she gently removed herself, rose from the desk and turned to face Joe. He had risen also and stood a few feet away gazing at her steadily, his gray-blue eyes darkening like the sea at dusk.

"You've been waiting a long time for some information about the murder. Are you ready to write your article at last?" Eliza asked, trying to read his thoughts.

Joe shook his head. "It's not my story."

Eliza was too weary to puzzle over his meaning. "Well, who's going to write it then?"

"You are," Joe stated.

Eliza blinked. "Excuse me? You want me to write the first article for your new 'Sleuth' column?"

"You're better qualified than me or anyone else to write this story," Joe asserted.

Eliza's tired brain woke up, as the idea took hold. "All right, I'll do it. Writing the article might be a good way for me to come to grips with the darkness of Fiona's murder."

"If you're willing to change your mind about being a newspaper woman, I've got a proposition for you," Joe said, surprising Eliza for a second time. "Your skill and tenacity in solving the murder impressed me. Plus, the stories you shared with me were excellent. How would you like to take over writing the column full-time? What with editing the paper and writing other columns, I'm overloaded as it is."

His remarkable eyes with their arresting, sooty lashes narrowed upon hers. "Of course, you'd have to attend all the Crime Busters' meetings."

Eliza met Joe's challenging gaze head-on. "If you're happy with the way I handle the first article, I'd love to take over the column. And don't worry; going to the Crime Busters' meetings won't be a problem. I might even make some new friends."